The Song of Horace

Squall Publishing
Seattle, Washington

THE SONG OF HORACE

une chanson de geste

by Allison McEntire

Printed in the United States of America

First Printing, 2014

ISBN 978-0-9833966-3-5

Squall Publishing
Seattle, Washington
squallpublishing.org

for Leslie Athens

ACKNOWLEDGEMENTS

Many thanks to the writing teachers who have guided me: Lynn Stowers, Kate Daniels, Tony Early, Erin Belieu, Robert Olen Butler and Sheila Ortiz-Taylor. Special thanks to Cate, John, and Kitty for their notes, proofreading, and friendship.

CHAPTER ONE

In the beginning humans lived forever and no one ever died. They all lived happily in a boundless garden at the end of the world, picking flowers and singing songs and trying not to interfere with one another's daydreams. It was only once death was discovered that anyone began the serious business of dying.

At that time there lived a princess named Angelica. Angelica was much like every other princess that ever lived in that she was wise and gentle and good and had flowing masses of golden blonde hair that made all the knights of the kingdom fall in love with her. Angelica was not stuck-up, however, and on May Day morning she rose before the sun, just like all the other girls, princess or no, and went beyond the walls of her father's castle and out into the meadow, barefoot, to gather flowers. This particular May Day morning the crocus and jonquils and early summer aster bloomed in a riot along the edge of the Forbidden Forest, and Angelica wandered, perhaps a tad unwisely, away from her friends and into a meadow covered in pale blue starlings. And there, at the end of a path that led to a dark thicket, she found an old, grizzled woman cursing and trying to wrench her walking stick from the jaws of a snarling, snapping dog.

"Let me help you," Angelica said, setting aside her bouquet of flowers. Angelica adored being helpful; she lived for it, which was fortunate for her father because without Angelica's help few things were accomplished in his kingdom. The old woman sneered at Angelica, kicked the dog, and went on trying to wrench the wooden stick from its drooling jowls. Angelica, in her wise and gentle way, leaned towards the cur and reached out to stroke its furrowed muzzle, but before a soothing noise had a chance to escape her lips, the old woman whacked her over the head with the walking stick and down Angelica dropped, unconscious.

When the princess awoke some time later, her flowers had scattered so much in the wind she couldn't retrieve them all, she had a nasty bump on her head, and the old woman had vanished. "God's foot!" Angelica swore, which was entirely out of character for Angelica, and, feeling sorry for herself, which was also entirely out of character, she slumped her shoulders forward and complained for the first time in her life. "But I only wanted to help!" she whined. Her perfect blonde curls drooped less than perfectly in her face. That, it occurred to the princess, had been the story of her life. Always helping and being perfect and thinking first of others, and where had it gotten her? She was the only princess she knew that owned more books than ball gowns. And on and on thoughts like these ran through the princess's mind as she made her way back across the field to the wall of her father's castle. "After all," she said to no one in particular as she shoved her way through the throng of peasants hauling their wares to market, "why should I care if my father doesn't? Why should I do anything if they're just going to find a new king?"

At that exact moment, Stupid King Mark (which was what all his subjects called him, more or less lovingly) was slumped down in his throne eating sweetmeats from a plate balanced on his fat belly and having a monstrously good time watching his councilors squabble, which was out of character for the king because his normal state was one of slumber.

"And I say dig a ditch all the way along the border, and post sentries at intervals, and at the very least we'll stop any cavalry-based invasion," said one.

"Poppycock," said another. "We've tried that twice already and both times it was a spectacular disaster."

"Alright, but what about fire?" said a third. They all stared at him as if he were mad. "No, seriously, we dig a long ditch, pump it full with tallow and make one immense wick…"

"If only the princess were here," sighed a fourth, and they all agreed that yes, it would be much better to wait and continue their discussion once Angelica returned from the forest, since she had a way of making them all see things so clearly. They would go instead now and have a nice lunch. But when the princess appeared she stormed past the throne room, shoved one of the councilors out of her way, and locked herself in her room. "Leave me alone," she screamed, and flung herself on her bed. She covered her blonde hair with one of her many goose down pillows to block out the polite but insistent raps of the councilors on her bedroom door. "Go away!" she shouted. "I don't care about your stupid line of defense!"

"Please princess," the council pleaded, but Angelica would not be moved.

"Go and find some other fool to run the kingdom," she screamed. "I'm retired!" And so the council left her alone, after some hours more pleading and cajoling and brandishing blandishments to no avail, all of them certain that without her guidance the country would fall to certain ruin.

Angelica, for her part, was enjoying the newfound freedom of being locked in her bedroom. She sat down at her vanity table and began brushing the curl out of her hair, one thousand strokes like the princesses in the storybooks, something she had never had any time for before that day. Her hair gleamed more brightly than spun gold. Her eyes twinkled in her vanity's reflection. "Shouldn't I have a veil of spun gold to drape over my eyes like a garment of sunshine, to protect my hair from fading in the afternoon light?" She talked to herself like that for hours, and then night came and the sun rose on the second day and she was no better than the day before, except in that perhaps she had grown even more vain and selfish in her sleep, dreaming of all the things she thought she should have. She ordered a breakfast of poached peacock eggs on a porcelain platter with a motif of satyrs prancing in the Forbidden Forest, hand-painted, and sent the kitchen staff into a frenzy. Her breakfast at last delivered, the eggs perfectly balanced in delicate cups at the center of the plate to best show off the handsome satyrs, paint still wet, she took one bite and pronounced it cold and sent it back with orders to do it all over, but this time make the satyrs less crude and crafty looking. When the king's china painter was told he would have to do it again, he nearly ran out to the edge of the wall of the castle to throw himself over and be done with it.

This was all fine and good for a few days, but after a few

weeks the country fell into disrepair. Stores of vegetables and slaughtered meats rotted in their storage houses because there was no one with the presence of mind to remember to send them to foreign markets. The crops failed, and the people were forced after a time to eat stale bread and bitter roots, and the people turned this bitterness towards the castle where they were still required to pay their taxes on the blighted grain because no one thought to pass an edict of relief. Rumors spread that the Duke of the neighboring city-state had mustered his soldiers on the border to take advantage of the situation, and some even whispered, in the dead of night and under the privacy of their own leaking roofs, that it might be for the best. Angelica, for her part, heard none of it; in fact, she refused to hear anything now that wasn't directly related to her own manifest glory. "After all, I am a princess, and a great beauty, and why shouldn't I demand my due?" she said to her mirror as she admired the fat emerald that now sparked on the middle finger of her right hand.

It might have been just as well that the Duke invade the country, and depose Stupid King Mark, and maybe shock some sense back into Angelica in the process, but the councilors had grown used to power and influence and comfort and would not give over so easily. They held an emergency meeting in the king's throne room, long after Stupid King Mark woke up to go to bed, and it was at this meeting the idea was first bandied about that the princess suffered from some sort of evil enchantment or maybe even a curse.

"It was a remarkable change in personality," said one as he flipped through an ancient tome borrowed from the alchemist, a cracking brown leather-bound volume so old the spine creaked like the trunk of an ancient, imponderable oak.

"She kissed my cheek on her way to gather May flowers," said another, "and the next time I saw her, she shoved me!"

"Those girls wander too far into the Forbidden Forest; I always said there would be trouble one day," said a third, only because he enjoyed reminding people he was right.

"See here," said the first, and he turned the book to show the other members of the council his discovery, "turn any sunny disposition frowsy with one quick incantation. It doesn't even require a cauldron."

"Naturally," said the second, "where would one get a cauldron on the edge of the Forbidden Forest?"

"I believe," said the third, disdainfully, "that is the point Alistair was making," and they fell again to petty squabbles, shoving one another across the broad oak table until Alistair fell back in his chair and the king's barber had to be brought in to clean and dress his wounded elbow.

"Then we can at least agree," it was at last decided, "that the princess suffers from an obvious enchantment, the cause of which must be discovered so that it may be lifted," as all enchantments have a corresponding antidote, if you only know which enchantment was deployed in the first place. "To that end, we propose," the council went on, each interrupting the other to add a bit here and there to the proclamation as the scribe's quill scurried back and forth across the paper, "that Stupid King Mark invest the noble knights of this kingdom… scratch that last bit and put 'King Mark' without the stupid, of course you have already… invest the noble knights of this kingdom with a quest to discover the cause of the enchantment, and by so doing provide the council with the manner by which it is to be reversed… are there too many bys in that sentence? Read it back again…"

At this point, had Angelica been herself, she would have kindly and gently pointed out, and in a way that was careful of each of their particularly fragile egos, that if the primary reason to reverse the spell was to prevent an invasion by the Duke, the sensible thing to do would be to send the knights to the border between the two countries, but Angelica refused to involve herself in such things now which was how the whole mess started, and so the council went on with its nonsense. "Read it back again… yes and put in a bit about a reward for the knight who returns as champion, let him have the princess's hand in marriage." The council all agreed it was a fine prize, considering it would be awarded after the curse lifted. One or two of the councilors even congratulated himself, in his own imagination, with the fantasy that he should win it. Angelica was, despite her blossoming vanity and her cruel new habit of torturing her servants with impossible demands, still very beautiful.

Stupid King Mark saw absolutely no flaws or impediments to the council's plan, and so between his naps he signed the edict. Soon trumpeters ran throughout the land blasting the news that the king commanded a quest, like the old days of his father, Lazy Michael. Riders posted the message far and wide, and before the Midsummer fires had burned down in each hearth every knight in the kingdom had taken up the quest.

Every knight, that is, but the Red Knight, in whose service a young squire named Horace now found himself most unfortunate. Horace was not the sort of young man that looked like he could be a knight. He was shorter than most men, almost as light as a girl, and his father was the dung peddler down in the Havershire market that picked his nose when he thought no one else was looking. Horace, ignoring great prejudice to his patrimony and person, had nevertheless managed to convince the Red Knight to take him into his household on the condition that he was expected to do just as much work as everyone else despite his small stature and unfortunate family, but now he was the most miserable squire in all the land because the Red Knight wanted there to be a war. He had refused to take up the quest, a decision that struck Horace as a deep dishonor to his vow of chivalry. Horace had never set eyes on the princess and had no interest in winning her hand for himself or the Red Knight or anyone else for that matter, but it was the first quest declared in his lifetime and he felt honor-bound to comply. On the third morning after Midsummer, Horace slipped from his master's stable and ran away as the sun rose over the Red River valley. He took nothing with him but a piece of flint knap in his pocket and a book of poems he'd picked up somewhere; indeed, nothing else belonged to him, and so with nothing off he set.

CHAPTER TWO

Horace knew he couldn't start out on a quest on his own. As he made his way along the red rock road between hill and dale beside the river valley, he told himself it would not be very difficult to find another knight to squire for. There was that unfortunate business at the King's tournament the year before when he tripped over the Red Knight's spear, but "No one will remember that," he told himself, and he shoved his hands in his pockets and whistled as he kicked a rock down the path a ways and jogged after it, kicking it again. "You are not that important."

Horace was right, in one respect; he was not very important. Of all the squires in the kingdom (by the account in the alchemist's archive it can be reckoned that at that time there were at least five hundred squires in Angleterre) Horace may have been the least important of them all. He had no great family, as previously noted, he had no athletic ability; in fact his physical strength was the least of his abilities. But Horace had something that made him a far more likely hero than any of the knights and squires of Stupid King Mark's court: small of stature, short on brains, Horace was made almost entirely of heart.

So it was, comprised almost entirely of heart, that Horace made his way from the Valley of the Red Knight, through the Pastureland of the Old Widow Haver, along the shire road and through the hay bales that lay rotting in the lane, to the edge of the Forbidden Forest which was cordoned off by a rough fence of split logs low enough for a small girl to hop over. Small as he was, he didn't hesitate to hop, even with the stories of his childhood threatening in the back of his memory. The Forbidden Forest was a terrible place packed with ghouls and goblins and all matter of troll sorcerers, which was why all the knights set out there straightaway. If anyone knew the cause of the princess's terrible enchantment, surely that creature resided in the Forbidden Forest with the other freaks.

"Knights of Angleterre?" Horace shouted from the forest side of the fence. A tortoise, all in all the size and shape of a painted porcelain breakfast platter, stuck his head out from underneath his hoary tortoise shell and blinked at Horace. The forest, silent as the grave before him, did nothing, for what with all its forbiddings and legendary danger, it was just a forest. "You there," Horace said, "have you seen any knights pass this way?" The tortoise looked at him again, blinked as patient creatures do, and retreated back within its platter-shaped shell limits, and that would have been the end of it except for Horace heard someone laughing, soft and high in the tree above him.

"Who's there?" Horace straightened up and peered into the thick canopy of branches, but the laughter faded on the wind. He wondered if he had imagined it. Determined to know for certain one way or another, or not to think of himself as a person who imagines things and scares easily (especially on the first day of a quest) Horace dragged together a stepladder of dead branches, flat stones, and one reticent tortoise so that he could reach the lowest branch and hoist his small body into the tree. As he climbed towards the source of the laughter, he looked out over the forest beneath him and discovered a clearing not forty lengths in that was lousy with knights. Littered with them.

They were, the Knights of Angleterre, at that moment engaged in their own impromptu tournament to determine who was strongest and bravest among them and therefore most likely to complete the quest. Aedger the Long of Tooth swung his spiked mace over his head and roared as Edward Pourtsmouthswitch fell flat on his face in the mud and muck of previous battles, and a terrible cheer rang out from the clearing that stirred the chattering blackbirds from their nests. Horace clung to a shaking branch and watched as knight after knight stepped up to face the red-faced giant, each one beaten back easily as though he were nothing more than a child. With each new victory, as the crumpled body of the defeated knight was dragged from the tournament grounds for recuperation or burial, the roar of the crowd of knights watching became more and more insistent. Horace shuddered. The spectacle raised the hairs on the back of his neck and the corresponding hackles in his very large heart, so he was busy contemplating why these men would waste so much time fighting one another when someone kicked the trunk of his perilous perch and Horace fell out of the tree, the source of the laughter that lured him there in the first place forgotten.

"What's this then?" A young man, no older than Horace, perhaps twenty, stood over him, examining Horace's ragged dung-peddler's coat with the tip of a jewel-encrusted sword. "Are you one of the faeries?" With brown ringlets of hair haloed by the curtain of light that pierced the canopy of the forest, the strange man looked like an angel. "Are you mute?" the man said.

"I am Horace, squire to the Red Knight. Well, until recently."

The man offered Horace a hand up, a hand braced in hammered metal plates that gleamed like the King's fanciest dinnerware, and Horace took it. "I'm Rollo. You're a bit shy of a squire," Rollo said, dusting Horace off as if he were a child.

"I am able." Horace scowled.

Rollo laughed. "Then you can be my squire. I have only just lost my squire to an unfortunate skirmish with an ogre, but he was never very bright and I'm sure you'll fare far better. Fetch my horse."

Horace didn't argue with the knight, or bother to explain why he was no longer employed by the Red Knight, as it didn't seem to matter to Rollo. Casting about for any sign of a horse, he ran off through the thicket towards what he imagined to be a wisp of white mane and a whinny. There was the horse just through the trees, tied to a rotten log, stripping bark from a nearby trunk with the skin of his teeth. Horace laid his palm on the horse's flank and it stopped chewing long enough to sneer at him.

"Fine fellow," said Rollo, when Horace returned with the sneering horse clomping along behind him, "although I must admit I hoped to find a faerie at my feet when I shook you out of the tree just now. I don't suppose you know anything about the princess's enchantment."

"Not yet," Horace said, "but I intend to," and Rollo clapped him on the shoulder as if to say 'good fellow' and held out his foot so that Horace could boost him up over the side of his horse. "I," Rollo told him, as they sallied forth into the Forbidden Forest, "have had much encouragement so far. I do not think this quest will be as difficult as everyone presumes. Martin, the Invincible Knight, for example, just yesterday was killed by a blow to the head, or was that the day before…" Horace ran along behind the horse, carrying the knight's broadsword on his back and listening as Rollo recounted the names of all the knights he'd seen die over the last few days. "That's the competition, young squire. Know your enemy." Rollo leaned over the side of the horse, twisted around in the saddle, and tapped the side of his head as if to indicate he was using it.

There was a sound like an arrow whizzing past his ear and Horace had barely enough time to jump back before Rollo, a rock embedded in the center of his forehead, slumped off the horse and fell to the ground at his new squire's feet, dead. Then Horace had barely enough time to shout bloody murder before another knight was upon them, armor black as the forge, his foot on Rollo's chest. "Surrender or die," the man threatened, and drew his sword.

Horace dropped Rollo's weapon.

"He was a great knight, was he? Renowned of bravery? Legendary of strength?" The Black Knight glared down at Horace. "Answer me!"

"I don't know sir," Horace said. The man's glaring eyes and booming voice made him want to run away. "I'd only been squiring for him a minute or two before you came along and killed him."

"Figures." The Black Knight sat on Rollo's chest, pulled a loaf of bread wrapped in cheesecloth from beneath the breastplate of his own armor, bit off a hunk, and chewed with his mouth open.

"He seemed to know a lot of dead knights." The Black Knight shrugged and went on chewing.

"I don't suppose you'd want a squire?" The Black Knight only glared at him, and so Horace said, "Alright then, I'll just be on my way." He started to back away, and the knight chewed on, content to let him go, but then he seemed to have a change of heart.

"Oh alright. Come back and build a fire," the Black Knight said. "I may as well rest here tonight."

"And I can be your squire, sir?" The knight nodded, and went on chewing. He went on chewing, and ignoring Horace, until he fell asleep.

The next morning Horace woke, stumbled down to the stream a few feet away, washed his face, and returned to the clearing with a pan of water for the Black Knight, only to find that someone had come along in the night and cut his throat, thrown his body over Rollo's just beyond the clearing, and made off with the horse and sword, both.

And so things went for many days. By the end of the first week Horace had followed seven knights all told, each one more dead than the last. Except for Lazarus, the seventh knight, who was currently perched atop his charger, sucking the meat from a walnut shell. "Mead!" he said, and held out his mail-bedecked arm.

Horace bit the cork out of his leather wineskin and held it up for him to quaff. "You are an excellent squire for such a small fellow," Lazarus said, and handed the wineskin back.

Together they rode through the forest, or the knight rode and Horace jogged just behind, and for the first time that week it was tempting for Horace to think they were actually getting somewhere. Lazarus was a pacifist and a vegetarian, and for several hours after Horace entered his service they'd drawn a wide loop around the tournament still roiling in the center of the forest, if only to avoid being drawn into it. Lazarus kept his distance. "A third of all knights die," he said, pushing aside a tree branch as he and his horse passed beneath it, "strictly on points of honor, and nothing ever gets done. Take the Grail Quest, for example. Why do you think the King had to make the table round?"

"Honor, sir?"

"Correct. Honor is the only thing our noble creator endowed us with in abundance and what do we do first off but try to horde it all from everyone else? Men are funny creatures," and he laughed and shook his head. They went on like this for several hours more, discussing honor and the nature of creation and time, when they came upon a boy tied to a tree, his mouth stuffed shut with the blue silk favor of some unknown court lady. Lazarus reigned in his horse, climbed down from the mount, and supervised the operation as Horace attempted to untie the child, but his kicking and squirming made the knots bind more tightly and Horace couldn't keep the poor wretch from thrashing about. After a while Lazarus suggested they remove the favor and a stream of expletives so foul poured forth from the downtrodden creature's mouth that I hesitate to set them down here, for fear of the Book Banning Committee of your local P.T.A., but rest assured they were the most delightfully foul words Horace had ever heard.

"Who did this to you, and why?" Lazarus demanded. The boy then launched into a second stream of expletives, this one far more foul and unsuitable for the school library than the first, and Horace was obliged to cover his ears for fear of his own scant honor, so he heard none of it.

Lazarus poked him in the back. "Yes sir?" Horace said, uncovering his ears.

"I said he's finished." He wore a funny little smile as he motioned Horace aside. One touch of the tip of his long sword to the principle knot that lorded over all the other smaller knots and the ropes fell away. The boy was soon running circles around them, kicking them when he could, and saying nasty things about their mothers. "Funny sort of creature, isn't he?" the knight said.

"How did you do that?" The knight only winked at him and held his foot out to be helped up over his horse. The boy, for his part, ran away.

But the boy was not forgotten like the laughter in the tree. The two men, the honorable knight and his barely competent squire, carried on unimpeded for a length or two before they were stopped again, this time by a roar of indignation that scared the blackbirds from their perches and made the flowers cower beneath their petals and hide their sunny faces. "Who ATE MY DINNER?" the roar-er cried, and Lazarus and Horace looked at one another as if to say, "it was nice to know you," before the giant was upon them and had one of them in each hand. "Well?" the giant bawled, his breath the fart of a thousand-year-old toad, "Which one of you was it?" He turned Horace upside down and shook him, and for once his small stature worked for him, for he slipped out of the giant's grip and tumbled to the ground. When he got up he kicked the giant's big toe, but it did no good. The giant held Lazarus between his thumb and forefinger to examine him in better light.

"I beg you to consider," Lazarus said, "that we didn't actually eat your dinner, rather we freed it, your dinner being a sentient being endowed by its creator with inalienable rights, the chief among those being not to be dressed and stuffed and served on a hand-painted platter..." and this seemed to work, for the giant was a reasonable, polite sort. He sat back on his haunches and listened to what the knight had to say. Once Lazarus had exhausted all philosophical arguments, he turned to poetry, all the while glancing at Horace and motioning towards his horse with his eyes. Horace tiptoed around the back-end of the giant and managed to catch the horse's reigns in his hands, but once there he had no idea what to do next, and Lazarus was in no position to tell him. Finally, the giant set Lazarus down between his knees, plucked his broad sword from the ground, and made it over to its rightful owner.

"Alright," the giant said. "You've convinced me. You and I are both equals in the eyes of the law. I could, since I am stronger and more able, take you for my dinner since you have deprived me of my own. But I am willing to be civil. We will settle this like men of honor."

"I suppose you mean a duel," Lazarus sighed.

"Naturally."

"Very well then. Squire, fetch another sword."

Lazarus gave the second sword to the giant, and the two of them squared off like equals, the giant giant towering over the average-sized knight, the massive war sword so small in the giant's hand that he held it between his thumb and forefinger and poked at Lazarus with it.

"At the ready." Horace watched in terror and glorious anticipation as the two fought for the right to eat the boy for dinner, even though the boy, as you remember, had already run away, and Lazarus was a vegetarian, and the giant didn't much like children anyway. Still, they both made an honorable show of it, and in the end, as Lazarus lay dying, which was the obvious outcome of any contest between a knight and a giant— I mean, what did you expect?— the giant bowed his head and said that the knight did him a great service. Heretofore he would live his life differently, so off he went to do just that.

Horace knelt beside Lazarus with tears in his eyes. "I have served so many knights this week, but you were the greatest of them all."

The knight, fading quickly, fixed his eyes on Horace, his voice serious and strong. "Take my sword, and my horse, and become me," he said, "and in this way I will finish the quest." And then he died.

CHAPTER THREE

Horace stared at the dead man for some time. It was as if all he ever wanted had come to him equipped with sword and charger; in short it was too good to be true. Still, Horace was not the sort of person to balk at the good gifts of fate. Soon he was unhooking eyelets and snapping loose the dead man's chainmail shirt from its sockets and wondering how on earth he was going to make the whole collection fit his diminutive frame. He didn't have long to wonder.

"A blacksmith could fit that for you," said a small, shy voice behind him. Horace looked over his shoulder to see the boy had returned, although since he was no longer cursing, it was hard for Horace to tell if he was indeed the same boy. "My uncle is the blacksmith on the far side of the forest," the child continued, inching closer, frightened of the dead knight's body. But he didn't run away.

"Well then, fetch some water for the horse, and we'll ride out to visit your uncle." It was the first command he'd ever given in his short life, but he was surprised by how quickly and effectively the order was carried out. Soon a stack of metal plates, a helmet, and a small assortment of sharp and pointed instruments of war were lashed to the horse's rear, just behind its saddle. Horace and the no longer-cursing boy led the magnificent beast through the undergrowth and down the dale, because, as lowly, insignificant creatures both, neither of them had ever learned to ride.

"It's a fine thing he did for you, dying like that." The boy skipped along beside Horace and had no trouble keeping up because they were roughly the same height and maybe the boy was a little taller. "Now there's a true hero. I watched it all from the hollow tree. That giant really gave him a wallop," and with this he popped his hand over the mouth of his fist and the smack reverberated through the forbidden trees. "I wouldn't have done it," the boy said and shook his head. "Dueling a giant is just dumb."

"He didn't die for me, he died for you. Show some respect." Now that he had been given his armor and his sword at the hands of a truly honorable knight, Horace felt far more seriously the weight of the quest on his shoulders. It seemed Herculean when one thought about it. If there were any enchantment on the princess, and it occurred to Horace for the first time that it was impossible to divine whether or not the princess was truly enchanted based on what he'd heard already about her condition, sudden personality change or not— if there were any enchantment at all on the princess, it was just as probable that the source of the spell had come from without the Forbidden Forest as within it. No wonder the other knights were caught up in contests to prove their fitness and ability. The tournament, and the rituals of challenge, these were things that it was possible to know.

"Say." The boy tugged on the ragged edge of Horace's cloak. "Why are you all running about in the woods anyway?" but Horace ignored him. Mixed in among the trees he saw the stones of a squat chimney and an acrid plume of smoke rising up from its mouth. His stomach grumbled. "My aunt will have pies. I'm going to eat at least seven." It was, Horace had discovered, not at all impossible to just ignore the boy. He went on talking regardless, as if he didn't notice his questions went unanswered, and he was soon enough distracted by a clump of wax he'd dug out of his ear, a black scorpion on a curling leaf, the ever-present, gentle nudge of the wind, or the sound of giants grinding bones between their molars that occasionally shook the forest.

"Uncle!" the boy shouted when the thicket finally cleared around the tiny, round stone house, so squat and so grown over with lichen and ivy it seemed to have grown up out of the ground. "I brought you a knight!"

The round door of the squat cottage opened and a woman, together with three otters, tumbled out of the entryway as if they had been leaning against it with all four of their right-side ears pressed to the door, when of its own accord, it decided to open and let them sort it out for themselves. "Auntie!" The boy tackled the woman as the otters slid on their bellies around them in the swept dirt yard. The otters were, it appeared to Horace, the family pets. After dinner the boy's uncle made them stand on their hind legs and clap the rhythm as he played Dixieland on a cigar box guitar, or maybe Horace dreamed that. He wasn't sure. The important thing was that the boy's uncle agreed to fit Horace's armor and promised to have it done before the end of the week.

"We can't let you lose too much time to these other rough fellows," the uncle said while he chewed on a straw reed. His wife turned her attention to sweeping cobwebs from a chiffon-robe piled high with books and dusty magazines as the blacksmith complained about the recent infestation of knightly-types throughout the Forbidden Forest. "Why, Jack Blackboots himself told me he'd come upon a pile of forty, all knights, killed each other one after the next and just fell on each other in a stack as pretty as you please, and you know if Jack Blackboots said it." With that the woman's shoulders shook and she dabbed at her eyes with her apron. "There, there wife, at least they're only interested in killing themselves."

"But the stench!" the boy's aunt wailed, and they all agreed that the stench that now hung about the forest like an early morning fog was unbearable.

"No matter, there is a limited supply of the chivalrous and they'll wear this quest out eventually. You," he said, and turned his attention towards Horace, "seem a sensible enough fellow. What do you plan to do once the armor's fit?"

Horace was ashamed to admit he didn't know. He jammed his spoon into his mincemeat pie and took another halfhearted bite, if only to fill up his mouth. "He doesn't have the foggiest," said his cursing, young companion. The boy's aunt and uncle looked to Horace for confirmation, and Horace felt compelled by honor to admit that yes, it was indeed true. He had no idea what to do next.

The boy's uncle chewed thoughtfully and watched the otters rolling over one another in a mass of brown fur at his feet. "If I," he said after some moment's consideration, "had no idea how to begin a quest, I believe I'd try to go and see Prester John." The aunt placed a pastry between them and a wooden bowl of clotted cream. "He knows everything that ever was, and everything that will ever be. If there's a way to achieve your purpose, Prester John will know it. What is," the uncle said, leaning forward and thumping Horace's chest, "the meaning of your quest, lad? Don't know that either?" he chuckled at his own joke. "That's quite alright, sonny, you might as well ask Prester John that too. Like I said, he knows everything."

"Well, there was that one year when the rivers froze solid in August and he didn't..." the boy's aunt said, and the uncle shot her a look that made her turn away from the table and busy herself at the fire, the hearth already gleaming from its lack of ash in contrast to everything else in the dusty, dim cottage.

"Well then, where is this miraculous person?"

"At the end of the world," the boy's uncle gestured east, gumming on his fork. "Ride towards sunrise, and you will find him." Horace had other questions, but the old blacksmith uncle told his wife to set the warming brick in the fire, he was ready to go to bed, and Horace didn't want to press the conversation further. It would take a few days to fit the armor to his tiny frame and learn to mount the horse, so there was time.

The armor, it turned out, was far less a challenge than the horse. The boy's uncle had instruments Horace had never seen before in any forge, and his gnarled, arthritic fingers flew quickly across his work. In a few hours' time, inches of chainmail were unraveled from the hem of the shirt and the long leg and arm plates were melted down, remolded, and set, a miraculous feat. The uncle seemed a bit self-congratulatory when he brought Horace into the shop for the final fitting with the family gathered around to admire his work. "He looks just like a little boy," said the boy's aunt, despite herself.

"He looks like a great fool is what he looks like." Horace had to allow that maybe the boy was right, but it mattered little to him what he looked like. He soldiered past them all in his iron exoskeleton, the joints fresh with oil and grinding against one another as they scraped and contracted, feeling very intimidating for the first time in his short life. The horse snorted and stamped his feet in the sandy loam, to add to the boy's derision. Horace saddled up beside the beast with his hands on his hips. "Oh yeah?" he said, staring up into the horse's huge black eye. "What's so funny?" He thought he'd swing himself over the horse's back, turn him around a few times in the yard and show him who's boss, but that was easier said than done.

As Horace soon discovered, in full armor it is impossible to mount a horse alone. One might get a running start, come up behind a horse and surprise it and in so doing leapfrog onto the horse's back, but when festooned in metal one's every moment was betrayed by the distinctive clink of joints popping in and out of socket. When one was in armor, and there was no guarantee of footstools or tree stumps nearby, one was forced to hold out his foot for help if he wanted to mount his horse; in short, Horace realized, perhaps for the first time in his life, a squire was a necessary, knightly accessory.

This unanticipated complication made Horace feel very, very foolish. He sat on a stump in the yard, sweating in the suit of armor, trying to puzzle his way out of his predicament. He could think of no one who was a squire himself that would condescend to help him; having received his arms from a dead knight, he wasn't sure he was even legally invested, and it had been his experience that one must be truly sure of an idea before trying to sell it to anyone else. He stood up then, put his iron-gloved hand on the horse's back, and attempted to pull himself up and over the flank of the horse and maybe swing his leg around… the horse balked, and Horace slipped and fell face down in the dirt.

Funny lad," the boy's uncle's said, watching Horace through the kitchen window. "Doesn't seem to know when to give up."

His aunt brought down a jar of dried pig snouts and began counting them out, one by one. "They say that princess is very beautiful," was all she said.

The two watched Horace most of the afternoon, trying and failing at mounting his horse, and by nightfall they'd had enough and sent the boy out into the courtyard to help him. "They say I should try to boost you up like so," he said and knit his hands together to make a basket of fingers, "with your foot here, you see? 'Surely if a man his size can serve a knight, a boy your size can serve a half-knight', that's just how she said it," the boy said, mocking his aunt's high, nasally way of speaking. "I think they just want to get me out of their hair."

Horace was certain that's what they wanted, but he didn't say so. Instead he held out his foot. The boy's strength was just enough to support him, and by working together they very easily put him on the horse's back. A faint cheer was heard from inside the cottage. "I suppose this means you'll be bringing me along to see Prester John," the boy said, hopping around the horse as Horace sat, befuddled by the reigns and bridle and saddle, on top of it.

"I'll think about it," Horace said, which of course meant that he would. What other choice did he have? He didn't know how far away the end of the world was, but he knew it would be futile to try and walk it in full armor. Since he didn't know how to ride, he'd need a squire to lead his horse. A child squire, he told himself, was better than no squire at all. Even a foul-mouthed, cynical little twerp like this one.

And so it was that by the start of the second week Horace set out in the full armor and honor of a knight to leave the Forbidden Forest and journey through the Desert of Unfathomable Nightmares to whatever lay on the other side. He sat up the night before in the cowshed, his sword plunged into the ground for a cross and a bowl of tallow with a rag for a candle, praying for a speedy conclusion to the matter of the princess's enchantment, be it by his hand or any other. The aunt said to her husband, when she roused herself at three a.m. to check and be certain Horace hadn't burned the cowshed down with his tallow lamp altar and foolishness, "You know, Henry? I kind of want him to win."

They set out the next morning: Horace, the boy whose name turned out to be Geoffrey, and the white war horse that Horace had named Lazarus because the knight had not had time to tell him the horse's name before he died. The Desert of Unfathomable Nightmares loomed ahead.

Meanwhile in the castle, long, long after the king's bedtime, the fat, drowsy monarch rolled over in his sleep and laughed. His laughter blew the curtains about in his bedroom, which startled a passing moth and swept it off its aerial path and thrust it, aimless into the night. Likewise the king's dreams flitted from course to course, beginning with dessert and culminating in a fine poached salmon stuffed with nuts and fruit, down the hallway the king always walked after dinner, through the window and into the night. In his dreams, the king could fly. He flew over the castle wall and into the sky, and hopped from tree to tree in the Forbidden Forest, laughing. In his dreams the king always ended at the same tree, the strange ancient tree at the edge of the forest, the one that grew up overnight with a sword in its heart. The king dreamed he could see the tree's heart, beating.

That same tree was the first odd thing Horace and Geoffrey noticed as they made their way past the cowshed and towards the edge of the forest. If they heard the sleeping king's laughter in the branches high above them, they did not say so to each other. "How do you think that sword got way up there?" Geoffrey asked, but Horace only shrugged and stood staring in dismayed silence at the desert wasteland that lay ahead. The wind whistling through clouds of red dust that rose in plumes above the sand dunes was the only sound at all beyond a wooden sign that had come loose from one of its nails and now swung, lopsided, in the wind: Beware of purple scorpions.

The length of the desert, according to the map the uncle drew for Geoffrey, was more than a three days' ride, assuming the best possible conditions. A man might expect to spend as much as a week wandering in the desert, and the horse could only carry enough water for five days. It was a depressing situation. Horace was not, however, as given to whining as most knights. "Look, we can't get lost; all we have to do is start out towards sunrise every morning. What could be more simple than that?" he said, leaning down from his high horse so Geoffrey could hear him.

"And the giant purple scorpions?" Geoffrey crouched down at the horse's feet to poke at a rock with a stick, half expecting to see one of the loathsome creatures skitter out from underneath.

"We're not getting anywhere worrying about them, are we?"

"I suppose you're right." Geoffrey stood up then, dusted off his hands, and tugged on Lazarus's reigns. When they crossed the border, leaving the ancient, mysterious oak behind, the three of them set foot into the longest week of their lives.

CHAPTER FOUR

The first and worst of it, depending on your perspective, happened three hours in. The desert was in no way cynically or sarcastically named: a wide expanse of deep red sand shot through with dark strains of smoky ash, the remnants of some great and far-ranging misfortune, beat in the sun like an open wound. Nothing lived for long in the Desert of Unfathomable Nightmares, but people were forever trying to forge a road through it, and it was the remains of an old work crew that gave them their first feverish dreams. The scene looked something like this: Horace, with Geoffrey puffing and wheezing as he led the horse and complaining about the pace, came to the crown of a high sand dune and saw in the valley below a camp large enough to hold sixteen men, gunny sack tarpaulins stretched over stacks of wares long since picked clean. Geoffrey ran down the hill with Horace hanging on to the saddle for his life while Lazarus tore off after him.

Geoffrey stopped when he saw the first mummy, a man leaning back against a post, mouth open, skin perfectly preserved by the dry desert wind. He wore a tunic of white woven cloth and a faded red sash that seemed ancient to Horace in his fine metal armor, and the knight wondered if the man hadn't been dead a long, long time. "The place is full of them," Geoffrey whispered, and Horace turned in time to see him draw back the flap of a camp tent, a woman sleeping, her arm curled around a small wooden doll.

"Do you think it was the purple scorpion?" Horace shook his head. "Whatever it was, it happened fast." Horace didn't say so, but a pit of fear and doubt was growing in his stomach. Whatever force had swept over the camp, it was entirely unknown. And, since there's no such thing as a purple scorpion, maybe he was right.

Horace and Geoffrey didn't know this, however, and as they shoved and tripped and stumbled out of the ghost town, their spirits were high, or a bit higher than usual, or a bit higher than within reason, truth be told. They'd had a fright, but they'd survived it, and there was not much on the horizon but sand. How could sand do them any harm? Horace let Geoffrey ride the horse as he took a turn at leading it. Soon Geoffrey settled into the comfort and luxury of being taken somewhere; he lay back on the horse's neck facing the road behind them, crossed one leg over the other, watched the desert disappear over the horizon, and felt very much at peace. He was just about to turn and say something to Horace about it when he noticed something odd. Horace had dropped the reigns. The horse was now plodding along between Horace and a figure the color of the shade cast by a rock.

"Horace?" The shadowy figure turned to look at Geoffrey. Beneath the hood of the scaly garment the figure wore, Geoffrey saw nothing. A blankness. Then, inexplicably, he had the strangest sensation that the blankness smiled at him. Geoffrey rolled over the side of the horse and landed with a crack in his knees. "Snake!" he screamed, and shot off towards the sunset in the direction they had come, the ghost camp and all the lay behind them.

"Snake?" Horace said to his traveling companion. A shiver

38

up his spine reminded him that he had no traveling companion, except for Geoffrey. Horace looked again at the figure beside him, but this time he saw things more clearly: a long black scaly legless beast stood next to him, the muscles behind his neck flared at eye-level. How the beast managed to project an image of humanity, Horace couldn't tell. He didn't wait around to ask.

"Snake!" he screeched, and tore off after Geoffrey, who was halfway back to the abandoned ghost camp by then but covering ground in half the time it took Horace, who had the misfortune of being fully ensconced in metal plate armor. "Hide!" he shouted, and dragged Geoffrey behind a tall sand dune. Only after a few agonizing minutes, and several more caught breaths, did Horace and Geoffrey dare to peek around. The snake, unclothed, the apparent enchantment completely broken, slithered around Lazarus in a circle, as if trying to make out from which direction to best try to swallow the horse.

"We can't lose Lazarus," Horace said. "If we lose Lazarus, we'll have to go back to get another horse, and I am not going back."

"You just ran five hundred and some feet back," Geoffrey said, but Horace ignored him.

"What kind of enchantment was that?" Horace said, instead.

"No magic to it, just demon snake. He spat a cloud of venom in the air, was all, and made us hallucinate. Demon snake are famous for their hallucinations. One time last summer a man came stumbling into my uncle's workshop with a demon snake draped around his shoulders. He said it was his wife."

"Hush." Horace peeped over the sand dune again. The demon snake had arched its spine and flared its hood to stand back up on its tail and stare the horse in its eye. Now was the time to act. Horace put his hand on the handle of his sword and slowly drew the sharp instrument from its scabbard at his hip. "Stay put," he said to Geoffrey, and he flew out from behind the sand with his sword raised high over his head, swinging as he ran towards the snake and the horse, screaming.

"Suit yourself." Geoffrey watched as the demon snake turned and hissed a longish stream of steaming red liquid from the back of its throat directly into Horace's eyes before Horace plunged the heavy sword into its throbbing snake heart, leaving it thrashing in the sand.

Geoffrey waited a good fifteen minutes, long enough for the snake to stop thrashing and for Horace to stop wandering around its carcass, sobbing and clawing at his helmet. At last Horace sat down on a small rock next to the snake's still body and stared glumly over the horizon, out at whatever came next, for neither of them knew what horrors remained between the point they had reached that day and the point at the end of the world.

"Feeling alright?" Geoffrey moved to reach out and touch Horace, then thought the better of it. Horace whipped his eyes towards the sound of Geoffrey's voice as if he had expected to find himself alone. A broad smile spread across his perplexed face. "Why, hello! You're that cursing chap, aren't you?" He reached out and tugged on Geoffrey's nose. "But where's Lazarus gone to?" Horace jumped up, cast about for his sword, and then saw it stuck in the ground through the heart of the snake and threw himself down beside it, weeping. "I've killed him!" he cried out, between choked sobs. "The only true knight I ever met, and I killed him!"

"There, there," Geoffrey said, embarrassed for him. "I'm sure he wasn't the only true knight," and Horace shot him such a look of cold disdain Geoffrey thought it better not to try and comfort Horace, and instead backed off a little and let him have a good cry.

"Oh why?!" Horace sobbed, grubbing up fistfuls of sand and watching it run through his hands. "All is lost, all is lost..." then he stopped sobbing for the moment and looked startled at the horizon. "Geoffrey!" he whispered. Geoffrey hopped up and ran back over to him, for the man didn't even remember his name a second before, so perhaps some sanity was coming back to him. Horace grabbed Geoffrey by the collar of his shirt and showed him the urgent horizon. He shook the boy when he didn't see. "Don't you see? Millions of them!"

Geoffrey squinted but saw nothing. He looked then at Horace with the hushed silence we afford the mad when they are in control of our situations, and finally Horace screamed, "giant purple scorpions!" and at least Geoffrey could heave a sigh of relief, for had there really been millions of giant purple scorpions flooding over the horizon, Geoffrey would have seen them. Instead, he decided to put Horace to work.

"Fire," he said. "That's what we need. Dig a ditch all the way around us, say fifteen feet, and fill the ditch with something flammable, light it on fire, and the scorpions will never get to us."

"Flammables." Horace let him go. "It's crazy, but it just might work." That was good enough for Geoffrey. He took a small ax from Lazarus's saddle bag and went to hacking away at the dirt while Horace ran off in pursuit of kindling from a huge oak tree he swore he saw not more than fifty feet away. Geoffrey thought that was a fine way to tire the mad man out, and soon enough they'd be back at questing, all this raving and sobbing behind them, so he went on digging. Horace returned half an hour later with a bundle of sticks and a very confused look on his face.

"See any giant purple scorpions?" Horace shook his head. "Did you reach the oak tree?"

Horace dropped the bundle of sticks down at the center of the circle Geoffrey had scratched out. "I think so. What for, though? I can't remember."

Geoffrey nudged the body of the demon snake with the ax. "Remember that?" Horace walked cautiously towards the limp snakeskin, pulled his sword from the snake's impaled heart, and wiped its blood away in the sand.

"It must have shot me in the eye just before I killed it," he mumbled.

"That's the first sensible thing you've said all morning." Geoffrey threw the ax out of the pit and climbed out after it, wiping his hands on his knees. Vultures circled overhead.

42

"I hope I didn't trouble you, overly," Horace said, sheepish and tired. He ran his sword back into its scabbard, kicked the body of the snake into Geoffrey's pit, and covered it over with sand. "I'm afraid I can't remember much at all… something about giant purple scorpions not being real," and then he turned back at the horizon and stared at it for several minutes, as if he had glimpsed a deeper truth than the one he could see currently, but couldn't quite grasp it in a way that translated into his current experience.

"Never mind all that. We've got some rotten princess to rescue, or some sort."

"Right, we have," said Horace, and he whistled for Lazarus, who trotted over amicably as if an episode of stark raving madness was in no way a hindrance to his faith in his master. "We best be on with it." He held out his foot, and Geoffrey boosted him up to sit on the saddle and took the reins. It was a strange site and a strange sight that they left behind them. Anthropologists argued for years in various scholarly publications about the weird circle cut into the desert floor, the dead snake body in its eastern-most position, and the bundle of sticks from a tree foreign to that environment placed atop it almost like a gravestone. Geoffrey chuckled to himself, imagining the future, as he led Horace and the horse away.

It was an uneventful afternoon, relatively, and Horace and Geoffrey were pleased to stop at a small brook that traced along their path east; Geoffrey stuck his head in the water by way of washing his hair. When he looked up again he said, "What kind of birds are those on the horizon?" Horace looked towards the black threatening mountains, closer and more threatening than ever before, and he made out a billow of red cloth just as it crested a sand dune and then plunged behind the horizon. A blue one, shot through with green jagged stripes, followed close behind.

"I think," said Horace, "and this is going to sound a bit foolish, given our environment, but I think those are people on holiday playing with kites."

Geoffrey said, "No they aren't," and went back to washing his face.

They walked towards the kites for the next half hour or so, distances being what they are in relationship to time, and soon they stood at the base of the hill staring up at the young men near the summit. A boy with pink hair and several metal rods stuck through his nose waited at the bottom of a nearby dune for the wind to pick up. He looked over his shoulder as they approached; no doubt he heard the clinking of Horace's armor and sneered.

"Say," said Horace, "are you quite alright?"

"What?" said the young man with the metal in his face.

"Are you laboring under some sort of curse?" Horace shielded his eyes and watched from his horse as the wind swelled the fabric of the kite and lifted the young man clear off the ground before depositing him back on his feet, three paces to the west and slightly higher up the hill.

"Go on, man." The boy with the metal studs in his face waved them away.

"Gladly," said Horace. "I don't suppose I can trouble you to point me towards a road that will take me through the Black Mountains swiftly."

The boy rolled his eyes, slumped his shoulders, and did all manner of things to suggest that the last thing he would ever consider doing on this earth was anything for Horace, but he dragged his kite down the side of the hill to point out the mouth of a little road that lay hidden between two dunes all the same. "I thank you, and the people of my kingdom thank you." Horace bowed, and his armor protested, loudly.

"Whatever," said the boy.

Their kites, there were at least seven young men with kites on the sand dunes that day, ranged over the heads of Horace and Geoffrey and Lazarus as they took the slow and winding path through the high-piled sand. "I wonder where those guys came from," Geoffrey said. Horace didn't say anything, for he was still recovering from madness, not yet certain which impressions were the lingering effects of the snake venom and which were his own. He had a strange impression now that those boys inhabited another time and place. And perhaps they did.

CHAPTER FIVE

By any reckoning they had made it through the Desert of Un-fathomable Nightmares alive. Horace hardly noticed, as the sand dunes gave way to porous black lava rock, that there were fewer and fewer nightmares to contend with. Geoffrey had to point it out. "And I didn't see one purple scorpion."

"Are you disappointed? We can go back," Horace said, but of course they didn't go back.

The Black Mountains are a formation of lava rock that had forced their way through the crust of the earth and split the land with jagged black teeth more than a million years before, and at the center of this ancient mountain range lay the Deepest Lake in the World, a lake so deep humans had never properly sounded its measure, and in fact had lost many scientific tools to the attempt to fathom it. No doubt the detritus of exploration lay at the bottom waiting for some industrious society to discover, preserved in coral, a veritable museum of mankind's fruitless attempts to master what their own civilization was destined to achieve— but that is for some book in the the future. What concerns us here and now is what Horace and Geoffrey saw when they stood on the western shore, for on the far side of the Deepest Lake in the World is the Most Beautiful Palace ever built. The trio, knight and squire and horse, stood at the foot of the world's deepest lake transfixed by the opalescent gleam of its ivory walls, reflecting the sun behind them from the not-to-distant shore. Just then something dreadful broke the surface of the lake, lashed its tail against a gently cresting wave, and shattered Horace and Geoffrey's illusions of a tranquil passage. Geoffrey almost reached out to put his hand in Horace's, then kicked sand at the surface of the water instead, nothing but ripples there now were terrible scaly fins had only just been. "Didn't you see that?"

"Didn't I see what?" Horace walked over to a canoe-shaped log and nudged it with his toe. The log, as it turned out, was just a log. Horace drew his sword and fished a length of kelp rope up from a pile of driftwood and storm run-off. Geoffrey said, "If you think I'm rafting across a lake with a creature like that in it, you're still mad." Horace threw the kelp at Geoffrey and he screamed and weaseled it off himself. There was nothing about for a boat. Horace sighed and stared at the high cliffs that swelled above the lake shore. He was beginning to wonder if he should just swim when Geoffrey started jumping up and down, kicking sand and pointing. "Look! Look!" Horace looked. On the far side of the lake, the two massive golden doors that were the entrance to the palace slowly ground open, somewhere trumpets bleated a fanfare, and Geoffrey shouted, "There's a woman, I can see her!" The doors parted. A woman in a long white trailing robe appeared at the castle entry, crowned by beams of light. She raised her hands to welcome them, and then, as she lowered her arms gracefully, a boat skittered out onto the water, bobbing towards them on the gentle waves.

The boat had a helm carved to mimic the curve of a swan's throat. It had eyes and a beak and proud spread wings that flared from either side of the boat as if it were a swan poised to take flight, and all over its graceful body it was covered with soft, white feathers. Unseen hands guided the swan across the water, and soon it reached the western shore where Horace and Geoffrey stood watching, mouths agape. Horace saw a tiny mechanism in the hindquarters of the swan, whirling, very much like the mechanism hidden behind the face of a clock, which must be what made it go.

Of course they accepted the invitation. Horace pulled back on one feathered wing and the boat opened like a door to admit the three of them, Horace, Geoffrey, and the horse Lazarus, who stepped daintily onto the boards of the swan as if he believed it were the creature's back, his hoof falls barely heard through the sound of water lapping at the boat's plump breast. Horace closed the wing behind them and knelt to wind the mechanism at the back near its plumed tail. The boat made a humming noise and rose as the tide started to turn itself towards the east. Soon they began the long trek across the deepest lake in existence.

The surface of the water was pure black. Geoffrey wanted to dip his hand in it. He imagined that the water was black like ink and would drip from his fingers and stain the feathers of the swan. He didn't dare ask Horace to boost him up so that he could lean far enough over the edge; indeed, if he had, it's not certain Horace was tall enough to do the job. The three of them, Horace, Geoffrey, and the horse Lazarus, watched the water skirt by underneath them, each of them thinking of the terrible tail that had broken the surface of the lake. "I wonder if it was a prehistoric beast. And if it eats squires," Geoffrey said.

Horace rolled his eyes. "Of course it does." Then he clapped his metal glove over Geoffrey's mouth. There was a shadow on the black deep, the faintest hint that something moved under the water.

Lazarus saw it first. The horse snorted, reared back on his hind legs, and paced his agitation back and forth while Horace and Geoffrey made soothing noises, patting and combing his mane. Lazarus would not be comforted. With a final defiant shriek he reared again and shot over the side of the boat and into the water. "Lazarus!" Horace screamed, but there was nothing to be done; the horse tried like mad to swim for the eastern shore of the lake where the ghostly woman waited, her arms stretched open wide, calling to him. In his wake the dark shade beneath the surface of the water grew.

Geoffrey leaned on the side of the boat, barely able to see what was happening before Horace yanked him back. "Don't watch," he said. A few moments more and the sound of water thrashing, the violent, terrible muffle of Lazarus's screams, then silence. Horace realized he was holding his breath, he wasn't sure why, and he was just about to release it when the terrible mouth of the immense creature folded over them and blocked out the sky. Horace, Geoffrey, and the swan boat were tossed over in a tidal wave of water as the creature swallowed. They followed one another down its throat in a swirling eddy that made them look a bit like toys being flushed down a drain. But somehow they were still alive.

The pit of the creature's stomach was pitch black until Horace stumbled against the boat in the darkness, ripped a few feathers off the starboard bow, and used his flint to strike up a torch. Geoffrey lay in a soggy patch of stomach acid that was rapidly burning holes in his green coat; Horace dragged him out of it and got the coat off him quick. Lazarus, a little farther down the creature's digestive tract, whinnied thin and weak.

"At least," Horace wiped one of his stomachjuice stained hands in the dirt on his armor and held the torch aloft with the other, "the horse is still alive."

Geoffrey stared at Horace in the flickering, stinking feather light. "Still alive? Can any of us count ourselves as still alive? Aren't we at the bottom of the Deepest Lake in the World? Haven't we been eaten?"

Horace decided this meant that Geoffrey felt better. He left him alone for the moment and walked across the creature's tongue or epiglottis or trachea, it was very difficult to determine exactly where inside the gigantic monster they actually stood, and reached through a hole in the muscular wall, took hold of Lazarus's reigns and coaxed the horse into the larger chamber. Lazarus was slick with digestive juices, and it took some doing to wipe him clean enough with the feathers he could cull from the swan boat, but the work was accomplished. Geoffrey held the torch.

"Now," said Horace, once the horse was saved from eminent digestion, "let's find our way out of here. We must be somewhere north of the creature's gullet." Horace turned toward the wreckage of their boat which was lodged against a wall of flesh so tight it seemed it should irritate the creature that had swallowed it. "If we can get the thing to open its mouth above the water... if he opens it below water then we're sunk." This was, let's face it, the far more probable occurrence. "If we can get the thing to open its mouth we might just walk out." Horace turned and looked at the boat again, and the flickering feather torch in Geoffrey's hand. It seemed like an idea had formed, which was fortunate because at that moment the sensation of descent rolled over on itself and the creature began to rise.

"Quick!" Horace flung Lazarus's reins at Geoffrey.

"What?" Geoffrey caught the reins and stood there holding the horse and the torch, trying to ignore the sickly warm water that dripped on him from the creature's throat.

"In the boat!" Horace stripped a few more feathers from the bird's breast and ran down the creature's throat towards his mouth, a fistful of feathers and little else but the flint and the book of poems in his pocket and the armor on his back.

Geoffrey crouched in the swan, held fast to the side, and waited. There was a roar and a rush of water and Geoffrey wasn't sure if he saw Horace slide past in the deluge that followed, but the next thing he knew for certain, after a blur of rolling over and smashing against things in the black water, was that he was lying in a patch of hot sand while a woman in a dress the color of the sky knelt over him, made him feel safe, and attended to his wounds.

Which were considerable. A gash the length and width of a pencil stained his shirt with blood. "Horace?" he shouted. The woman told him to be silent, not to bother himself, for all would be well with time. He struggled to try and sit up, but the woman laid a cloth over his eyes and coaxed him to lie down again. "But Lazarus," he said, and she responded calmly that she would give him a new horse, and it was then that Geoffrey decided all was lost. "Horace is dead and you're not telling me," he mumbled. The woman whispered that all would be revealed with time. Sleep. She pressed the mouth of a small bottle to Geoffrey's lips, and he drank, and slept, and when he woke again he was in a comfortable bed, lavish with pillows, the midday sun at the window reflecting like a thousand shimmering scales on the surface of the lake.

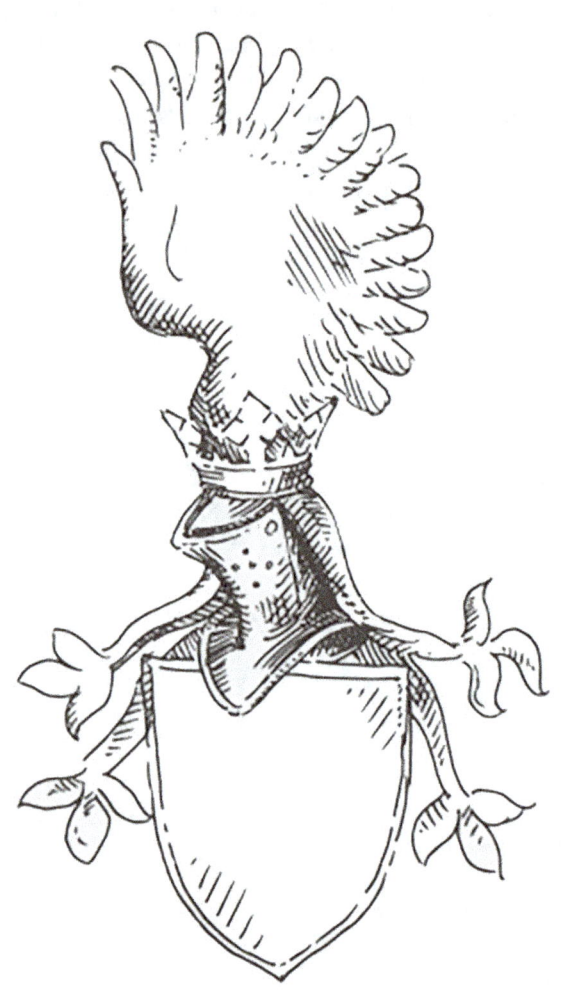

CHAPTER SIX

"Horace?" Geoffrey was alone in the room. There was no one there to tell him what became of Horace, so he slipped from the cushy mattress and nearly broke his leg on the fall— but the door was locked. There was no other furniture in the room, save the bed, which left Geoffrey trapped in a luxury of flounce, goose feathers, and ribbons. He kicked the door, but if that had any effect on the locked door's willingness to open, it made no such sign to Geoffrey.

Horace awoke with the dull ache of knowing that Lazarus was indeed dead. There was nothing more that might be done for him. A knight on foot was barely a knight at all, but Horace put that thought away and closed the curtains of his window on the inky black lake. Only then did he realize that he was not alone in the room.

A woman, older than Horace by ten or fifteen years, sat in the corner beside the bed, merely watching, calmly watching. "Forgive me," Horace stammered. "I…" but then nothing occurred to him to say. She waited for him to finish, her hands long and thin and folded in her lap. At last Horace made a short, frustrated bow and took a step backward. "I am Horace, at your service Lady." She smiled, and Horace was struck dumb by the whiteness of her teeth. They looked like baby's teeth, each one small and perfectly positioned. Everything about her was perfectly positioned and gleaming. Then she opened her mouth to speak.

"Lie down and rest, get your strength back. Your doctor will be very angry with me if you don't." Her voice had the pleasant undertone of a crashing wave— but Horace couldn't be coddled and lose time. For all he knew, the war had already started and his country was now no more than a hunting preserve for the Duke of Loraine.

"Where is my armor? My squire? Where's Geoffrey?"

The woman smiled, stood, and put her lovely hand on Horace's shoulder. She was more than two feet taller than he was; when she looked down at Horace and stroked his cheek she seemed almost motherly. "Please," she whispered, "your doctor will be very cross with me. I will tell you everything if you lie down."

"But the quest…"

"In time, there is more than enough time, just please, lie down." Horace looked through the window again at the shore of the lake, the swan boat busted on its side in the sand. Just a few hours more, to humor them, Horace thought. He let himself be tucked in again. The woman smelled like a June morning when she leaned over him, her hair brushing his cheek, soft like fresh-spun silk. "That's better." She put her hand on his forehead and smiled, the sunlight gleaming through her hair.

"How long have I been here?"

"A few days, nothing more." She waved her hand as if to

dismiss all unpleasant thoughts of lost time and the fate of the kingdoms. She brushed his hair out of his eyes. Then she leaned down and kissed him in the center of his forehead like a mother might kiss her child. "Your armor is being cleaned and polished as we speak. And your squire is enjoying the same treatment as you, in the room next door. I'll bring him in to see you, if your doctor agrees."

"Say, there's nothing really wrong with me, is there?" Horace struggled to try and sit up again but the woman urged him back with her soft words and perfect smile.

"Nothing serious. Rest." She reached for a bowl on the bedside table and brought it to his mouth, cradling his head in her hand and urging him to drink. Steam rose from the broth even though the bowl had been in the room when he woke up, and he didn't know how long before that.

"What is it?" She coaxed him into a sip. The hot liquid flooded his throat and his senses and soon he was asleep again. The beautiful woman, she really was a beautiful woman and not just the sort charming enough to bewitch Horace, rose from his bedside, her work done, took the bowl of warm liquid sleep with her, and left Horace dozing in the mountain of pillows. And so things went for several days.

Geoffrey, meanwhile, was having the time of his life. The castle's inhabitants were all truly beautiful people, and they made Geoffrey their mascot, carried him around on their shoulders, and put him in the seat of honor during the nightly feast. The men—there were many men in the Most Beautiful Palace in the World—

made him the captain of their sports league. Every morning when they played their games in the courtyard for the delight and entertainment of the women, Geoffrey sat on a golden throne above a raised dais and shouted at the referees when he didn't like their calls while the women brought him fruit and candies and braided flowers into his hair. The one black spot on the whole experience, for Geoffrey, was that they wouldn't tell him what was wrong with Horace. As he watched two men engage in the wrestling ring, arms locked, muscles straining as they grunted and tried to throw one another over, he remembered with a sinking feeling his own distinct impression, from that hazy morning days ago when they first stepped into the swan boat, that they were a sort of sacrifice and were meant to be eaten by the beast. As for the beast, no one ever spoke of it, and when Geoffrey looked out over the placid, inky lake, it was hard for him to believe it even existed.

"Hey," he said, on the fifth morning of his stay in the World's Most Beautiful Palace, "didn't one of you say I could visit Horace?"

"Of course! After the tournament. He will sleep until at least mid-afternoon." The tournament came and went with about as much fanfare as you expect from a tournament, and Geoffrey asked to visit Horace again. "Let another hour or two pass, his doctor has only gone in just now to see him. Have another slice of cake."

On the seventh morning Horace waited until the detail of nurses came in to change his sheets. He pretended to sleep until one came close enough to pop a thermometer in his mouth, smacked her away with his goose down pillow, and ran out the door in the confusion of shouting that ensued. He ran through the castle corridor to the feasting hall and would have run out of the castle and left Geoffrey altogether had he not happened to peek in on the great hall and glimpsed his squire at the head of the banquet table, sitting on the lap of the woman with hair the color of the sun. In the flickering torchlight it seemed to Horace that she sometimes wore the skin of a haggard old crone. A touch of winter came into her appearance, and it chilled him.

"Horace! You're awake!" Geoffrey banged the table several times and insisted Horace come sit beside him at the high board. Everyone else in the room, the hundreds of ladies and gentlemen, all of them spectacularly beautiful, stared at Horace with disdain. Without his armor, he was even more short and common-looking than ever.

The woman with the hair like sunshine raised her hand to silence the crowd. "His name is Horace and he is our honored guest. Let him approach." Horace had an unpleasant thought that everyone was laughing at him as he made his way through the crowd to climb the satin-draped stairs. Geoffrey beamed down at him as if he had conquered this territory himself, and now invited Horace to pay fealty to his liege. Horace was not so impressed, but his stomach growled as he mounted the stairs to the great banquet table and there was no denying that after four or five days of restorative soups and beef teas he was ravenous.

After the fifth course, he put down his fork. "Where is my armor and where can I buy a horse?" he said, very plainly, to the charming, sweet-looking woman to his left. She wore a veil of silk so thin it appeared to be spun from spider webs, and her large blue eyes pooled with sympathy for whomever she favored with a glance.

"You are a knight?" she whispered, in a low, inviting way that had the peculiar effect of causing Horace to want to lean towards her, the better to hear her. It didn't hurt that his head then filled with her charming, delicate scent.

"I am," he said. "I received my arms from the honorable Knight Lazarus just before his death." Horace shifted in his seat, but the woman didn't seem to disapprove of the manner of his investiture, which cheered him, and he found himself telling her a great deal he might have kept to himself. When he heard himself say, "Prester John," he blushed and murmured something about how kind she was to listen to his ambitions, but the woman brushed the last bit aside with an enthusiastic smile. She put her hand on Horace's forearm and squeezed it.

"You must be careful as you approach Prester John's kingdom," she said. "It is very nearly at the end of the world and you might fall off if you aren't careful."

"Does the world really just end like that?" Horace leaned closer, whispering, his forehead almost touching hers. The woman frowned. "Oh yes, at least I've never seen it for myself, but I've always been told, ever since I was a little girl, on no account to go near the end of the world or I might just fall off."

"I wonder what happens if you do fall off?"

"You just fall through space forever. At least, that's what

my mother told me."

"Your mother must be a wise woman."

"Oh she is, very wise. Would you like to meet her?" She raised her cup and nodded to a woman on the far side of the high board who had the same spun gold hair and sweet expression. The woman smiled and nodded back. They could have been sisters.

"How old is she?" Horace was more naïve than rude, and to his good fortune, that was the way the question was taken.

"Oh no one knows," she said. Then she lowered her eyes and whispered as quietly as she could: "Everyone says they can't remember, but I was trying to the other day. I think I must be at least three hundred years old." She stopped then, looking into Horace's eyes, searching for his reaction. Horace stared back at her, not sure whether she'd made him the brunt of her joke. "I must be mistaken," she said, and sipped her wine. She seemed disappointed. After a few minutes of silence she said, "That can't be right, can it?"

"Maybe it only seems like three hundred years. You should come with me and see the world a little."

"Why would I ever leave the palace?" The woman turned away from him as if he had suggested something offensive. Geoffrey leaned on his right arm and said, "Having a good time?" Horace scowled, and Geoffrey clapped him on the back. "Stop worrying and try to enjoy yourself. Duty, honor and Angleterre, that's all this one ever thinks about, isn't it Horace?" Geoffrey climbed onto the banquet table and the men and women laughed and clapped as if Geoffrey's bad manners were the most delightful thing they ever witnessed. "Duty, honor and Angleterre!" Geoffrey shouted, and danced a jig around the congealed salad.

"Stop that, you look ridiculous." Horace glanced around to see if anyone agreed with him, but everyone else clapped louder and shouted suggestions for Geoffrey to act even more ridiculous. The woman at Geoffrey's left, the one who had been at Horace's bedside the first morning, watched with the sort of barely disguised glee one reserves for watching tragic acts of embarrassment when one is absolutely alone. In that moment, her face was so contorted by schadenfreude, a kind of pleasure we sometimes take in the misfortune of others, that she looked ugly. Horace leaned towards her, and her eyes cut at him as if to warn him to back off, then softened into a sugary smile as her wrinkles melted away. "When will my armor be ready?" he said to her.

"A day or two." She looked away. But Horace would not be blown off.

"I want to see it. Have someone take me to see it."

"Oh alright," She rose from the table, Geoffrey's dance now over and Geoffrey happily tucked into an immense trifle. "Follow me."

As Horace followed her through the Most Beautiful Palace in the World, this is what he saw: a courtyard made of stones so white and gleaming Horace thought it must be carved from one enormous pearl; a shrine to poetry covered in ivy and lilies and tiny purple flowers that bloomed whenever the shrine was touched; a miniature of the palace painstakingly decorated with such intense detail it seemed that the dolls were moved each day to reflect one or more of the day's events; a stable peopled entirely by stunning black stallions; a grove of trees that grew their own lighted candles; a room decorated by the wind. By the time they arrived at the armory he was out of breath, but the woman with hair the color of the sun stood waiting for him to push open the door.

What he saw inside took his breath away. Armor stacked floor to ceiling with only a tiny window at the very center of the back wall for light, and a small fire that roared behind the blacksmith's table day and night from the look of the grime on the furnace. The blacksmith, Horace realized as he watched in amazement, was a mechanical man made entirely of clockworks: an automaton. There on his table was Horace's breastplate, emblazoned with the arms of Lazarus, a mighty oak tree on a field of white. "Hello Vulcan," the woman said. The mechanical man stopped his work, raised his arm, waved, and then opened a bottle of linseed oil and poured some out onto the clean cloth in his hand. Horace watched as the automaton spread the oil over the breastplate, revealing the shine beneath the layer of salt water, sand, snake venom and blood. "When will Horace's armor be ready, Vulcan?" The mechanical blacksmith held up two fingers. "See, there you go. You can leave in two days."

She made some excuse, she had a headache or something, and sent Horace back to the feast on his own. Along the way he came across the miniature palace again and stopped to peer through the tiny stained glass windows. The figures themselves didn't move, but they seemed frozen in their most recent position as if Horace had come along and stopped their movement just by his observation of it. But even odder yet was that the people all seemed to be exactly where they really were, or at least were Horace thought they were. Geoffrey was— and Horace couldn't help but laugh when he saw Geoffrey— a tiny mannequin of perhaps half an inch, sprawled out on the dining table sleeping, the other diners talking over his full belly. The woman with the hair like the sun sat staring through the window of someone's bedroom, possibly her own. Horace wondered if the purpose of the doll house was to serve as a map of sorts. A map of being. The automaton in the foundry was hunched over his work, but the object on his table represented, as far as Horace could tell, a small mechanical unit that in no way resembled his own breastplate. Had he been a modern man, Horace would have thought the object looked more like a bomb. Horace shivered and turned away. It would be impossible to have every detail in place at every moment, and yet somehow someone had accomplished something very nearly that. To test his theory, Horace turned away from the doll house map, counted to forty-nine, and then turned back again.

Everything was exactly as before, except for in the courtyard of the stable, where a man had appeared leading a horse. The horse was the only beast in the stable that was gleaming white.

CHAPTER SEVEN

"Where have you been? There's a play in your honor, the girls have been practicing for weeks." A man in a formal tuxedo coat came around the corner, found Horace about to touch the small felt horse in the center of the doll house stable, and grabbed his arm and shook him.

"Weeks?" Horace said, in alarm, and the man shook his head and laughed. "Days, days, of course. Come this way." As the man dragged him around the corner, Horace wanted to pocket the miniature Lazarus, but that would be stealing. He felt a little better when he realized that if he took the horse he'd no longer see it on the map. The miniature Lazarus watched as he walked away.

The play was about Sir Gawain's limitless patience. Horace drummed his fingers on the arm of the ornate wooden throne they brought for him and made all manner of rude sighs and even rolled his eyes in places when the pacing dragged on. Geoffrey had to ask him to behave. In the final act, when Sir Gawain is rewarded for his great patience, Horace sprang from his seat and pushed his way through the reception line to run back to the hallway where the doll house occupied a corner, unobtrusively, as if no one had thought much of it for years.

Geoffrey followed Horace into the corridor to give him a piece of his mind. "There's a party in there in your honor. I think you're being rude."

"Yes, but why Geoffrey?" Horace said, tugging on the roof of the doll house stables to see if it would snap free. It didn't.

"How would I know why? You've been grouchy since we came here. I think you're resentful that I'm so well liked." Geoffrey folded his arms across his chest. "Why are you messing with that? It doesn't belong to you."

"I mean, why is there a party in my honor? And why now?"

"Why not? You don't want anyone to have any fun is all."

"Because I'm on a quest!" Horace shouted, and his arms flailed as he whirled around and knocked the tower off the eastern wing of the toy palace. Tiny bricks and straw and ancient portraits skittered across the real palace floor. One of the portraits, only half painted, was of Horace, and it rolled to a stop at the toe of Geoffrey's shoe.

"Sorry. I forgot about the quest." Geoffrey knelt to pick up the miniature portrait. "Say look, isn't that a picture of you?" Horace took the portrait and held it up to the light. In the diminutive frame, just as gilded and ornately carved as any frame in the palace, was an oil painting of Horace so small that it must have been done with a single bristle of hair rather than a full-sized paintbrush. Only half the face had been completed, as if Horace surprised the artist in the act of creation when he demolished the tower. At the bottom of the frame, a curious emblem: On the sixth day of the sixth week of the year of unbridled selfishness. Horace turned the miniature over, but there was nothing on the back, so he turned it over again and read the emblem out loud. "Maybe that's some kind of date," Geoffrey said.

Horace put the miniature on the edge of the table by the doll house and peered through the hole left by his own rough destruction. Past the lords and ladies dancing in the ball room, and all the rest feasting in the great hall, Horace could see that the woman with the hair like the sun sat at the high table, whispering to another lady behind her fan. "They are always conspiring here." Geoffrey could do not much else but agree. Then Horace saw what he was looking for.

Lazarus had been led through a large stone corridor behind a man Horace had never seen before. They seemed to be working their way down a series of tunnels beneath the palace. Horace traced their path backwards along the stone hallway until he found the doorway very near the mechanical man's foundry that opened on the labyrinth. "What are you going to do? You can't just go down there and point out to the man that it's your horse. They know it's your horse. They just don't want you to know he's still alive for some reason."

"I don't know. I'll worry about that when the time comes." Horace turned away from the doll house, its seductive feeling of control, the shrinking of the known world into one in which it was possible to know exactly where one's enemies were at all times. He stared at the broken tower. "I'm going to go up to the tower and see if there's a portrait of me there," he said to Geoffrey. "You can come along if you want."

Geoffrey did go along, but only because he wanted to be there when Horace realized he was acting like a ninny. "It's all prophecies and poetry with these people. They probably want to make you king or something. What's so bad about that?" Horace ignored him. When they reached the door to the tower in the eastern wing, it was locked. Of course it was. Horace kicked the door, but that only made his foot hurt. Then he peered through the key hole, but whatever he saw there he couldn't make much sense of, only what looked like a round blue eye staring back at him. "Maybe we should ask for a tour."

"Maybe," said Horace, as if he wasn't really listening. Then he looked up and noticed something very curious. "Geoffrey, can you see that hole in the ceiling there? Climb up on my shoulders and look, tell me what you see."

With little effort, the squire stood on the knight's shoulders and squinted at the hole in the ceiling, maybe three and a half feet above Horace's shoulders, but it was enough. "The tower's gone," Geoffrey said. "Like it just blew away."

"That's impossible." Horace craned his neck, stretched, put Geoffrey down so he could jump up and down and get a better view, but he was just too short to see anything. He slumped back against the wall. "It's hopeless," he said.

"What's hopeless?"

Horace waved his hand around his head. This. Everything. All of it. He did not, it should be noted at this juncture, say 'I give up'. Geoffrey only scowled. Over the past week, even if Horace had spent most of it sleeping, Geoffrey had gotten to know the people and the palace and maybe they were a little strange, but what wasn't this side of the Forbidden Forest? They were good enough people in his book. And anyway, he liked being the center of attention. "Look, I'm sure if you talk to Constance…"

"Constance?"

Geoffrey laughed. "Constance. I think I've heard you refer to her as the woman with hair like the sun. She's not a goddess, you know, just a nice ordinary lady. Tell her about the quest and ask her what they want with our horse, and when we can leave with him." But of course Horace couldn't do that.

Horace woke the next morning in the warm bed in the high tower on the western wing where he'd woken the first morning, only this time no one sat in the chair beside him, keeping watch. No bowl of warm soup waited on the bed stand for him to drink. The curtains had been drawn back, however, and in the dawning daylight he could see across the castle keep to the far eastern tower. It was all there. In fact, it looked more pristine than usual, as if it had been skillfully rebuilt overnight. And in the courtyard below his window, a man led Lazarus in the open by a gold tether. Bells jingled in his bridle. Horace jumped out of bed and ran to the window to shout down at the groom but no sound came out of his mouth. The man put Lazarus through his paces, then led him back towards the barnyard and Horace could do nothing to stop him. He grabbed his shirt, pulled it over his head, and ran out into the hallway in a panic. He didn't see the tiny portrait of himself, so small it could fit on a postage stamp, propped on a tiny easel on the table by his bed.

The man in the courtyard had vanished by the time Horace reached the stable, and so he went stall by stall looking for Lazarus. The stalls seemed to stretch on over the horizon and into infinity. The stable was deserted when he started, but when he finally gave up and turned back it was teeming with people. Men in red livery that reminded him of the squires and servants of the Red Knight's household ran back and forth from the tack room to the palace. One stopped him with an officious, arm's-length attitude. "Just where do you think you are going?" he said, sneering at Horace. Horace opened his mouth to speak, but no sound came out. He clutched his throat and gagged. "I'm sorry," said the man. "Could you repeat that?" Horace kicked at the dirt, the way Lazarus did when something frustrated him, and cast about for a better alternative. There was a chalkboard in the tack room, but no chalk. Horace stooped in the dirt and started to write in the sand.

"I saw my horse," he wrote. "White stallion. Help me find him."

The servant turned on his heel and headed off in the opposite direction. "Best of luck to you," he tossed over his shoulder as he walked away.

"Having a tough morning?"

Horace turned around and there was the woman with the hair like the sun, or Constance, whichever you prefer. She stood in the low stable light with her hands folded demurely together, so calm and statuesque. Horace sort of clutched his throat, lame and mute. He could barely call himself a knight without his armor and his horse, but how could he complete the quest without his voice?

70

"Cat got your tongue?" She put her arm around him and led him towards the courtyard and out into the light, and soon he felt the soothing ease of surrender. He limped along beside her, forlorn, as she dragged him away from any chance of Lazarus, for that morning at least. "What a bother is language," she said, as if to herself exclusively, when they reached the physician's door. "I think I might be happy not to worry with it any more. Maybe you should consider yourself lucky." Horace pleaded with her, with his eyes, and she sighed. "Alright then, if you insist." She pushed open the door.

The doctor's office (Horace had never seen the office or its doctor) was stacked high with books. One great tome lay open beside what appeared to be a surgery table; besides the table and the desks there were no other furnishings. There certainly were no instruments or sterilization equipment for these things were not yet known even in the imaginary world, but the overabundance of books struck Horace as symptomatic of the lopsidedness of the world he and Geoffrey had stumbled upon where value and emphasis were placed in the wrong things entirely. Not that Horace thought there was anything the matter with books.

Constance took a look around for the doctor, and, finding none, went to the large volume open next to the surgery and began to read in a strange, whispering voice. It was not a language Horace recognized. After a while he fell to running his fingers over the covers of the volumes closest to him and tracing the gold lettering and strange wispy print that decorated their spines. "Here is it," Constance said, snapped her fingers, and whispered a foreign and improbable phrase three times. "Now speak."

Horace meant to ask what it was she wanted him to say, but another phrase altogether came from the pit of his stomach in a low, gravelly voice he was certain did not originate from his own body. What he said, although he couldn't understand it himself, was, "The old world must make way for the new." Constance looked at him with her brow wrinkled in worry; clearly she understood no more of this than Horace himself. He smiled at her, feeling lame again. "Say it over," she said, then she leaned against the lectern with her arms folded and her back to the magic book and glared at him. "Why did you come here?" she said, after several clumps of sand had slipped through the immense hourglass on the high shelf against the wall that, covered with dust, looked like it hadn't been turned in months.

Horace meant to say, "I'm on a quest," but what came out was, "to heal the rift between time and space." This seemed to enrage Constance, and she turned her back to him again. "Please," he tried to say, "just let me have my horse and I'll leave," but what Constance heard was, "beauty and peace cannot belong to you alone, Angelica," which was odd because that was the princess's name, and Horace had never heard the princess's name before. No matter, he could hardly form the words to ask what it meant. Every time he tried, what he heard was something stupid like, "When is supper?" which he knew perfectly well was at sunset, and "Who will win the Stanley Cup?" which meant nothing whatsoever. Constance ignored him, furiously turning pages. Then she stopped and was very still and very quiet, like a hawk watching and being watched, for a very long time. When she spoke again the light was much higher in the sky and Horace had the uncomfortable notion that he had fallen asleep against his own will.

"You should be able to speak normally now," was all she said to him, before she pushed open the heavy wooden door and stepped out into the gleaming cobblestone courtyard. "Your horse and your armor and your squire are waiting for you in your room. Collect them and go." And with that, she left him there, alone.

Horace sat staring at the hourglass until he was certain she'd gone, then he slipped out into the courtyard and made a run for it. When he reached his room he flung open the door, but it was empty. That isn't to say it was devoid of all objects; the bed, smartly made, showed no signs of hoof prints or horse nuzzling in the blankets; the closet, stocked with clean undershirts, pressed slacks, and starched collars, didn't gleam at any corner with polished metal. Everything was exactly as he left it in the morning; well... cleaner and less lived in, except for the miniature portrait on the bedside table. That, Horace realized, was very different. Horribly so. In the time it took to walk with Constance to the doctor's office, listen to her read the spells, be knocked out and brought back, which was oh just under three and one-half hours, some tiny, unshakable hand had come along and finished the portrait. Horace picked it up and stared at it. In the portrait, the armor he'd received from Lazarus the knight was propped up on a chair like a seated person, while Geoffrey and Lazarus the horse stood on either side looking unnaturally serene. Geoffrey's expression in particular was one of self-satisfied bliss. Horace put the postage-stamp sized painting in his pocket with the book of poems and the shard of flint. These were the only things he took with him when he left the Most Beautiful Palace in the World.

He climbed down the black rock at the eastern wall of the castle for days, picking his way through loose stones and broken ladders left a millennium ago by primordial travelers and other desperate refugees of the world's most beautiful palace. The sun was larger on this side of the world; often it was hard to keep his eyes open or otherwise avoid weeping. He kept the miniature in his pocket but didn't look at it for fear that the picture would draw out more tears than the sun. On the horizon, when he shielded his eyes with his arm and dared look ahead that far, he could see a thin, slate gray line that seemed to stretch from one edge of the world to the other, and beyond that only the empty sky. There was nothing else to do but walk toward it.

So Horace walked. Without his armor he was lighter and his limbs moved more easily and walking was more enjoyable than it had been since his quest began, a heavy weight lifted from his shoulders. Horace had to laugh; armor really was a heavy weight, and so far it had protected him from precious little. It certainly didn't do much for Lazarus, or the other knights Horace followed before him. Perhaps, and this sort of thinking was something akin to blasphemy for a person of Horace's age and extraction, perhaps the only real use of armor was to make it plain to all that one was a knight. Out here on the plodding road, alone, that made no difference at all. He was lucky to be rid of it, Horace decided.

And the horse! A horse would certainly help matters now, it was hard to deny, but there wasn't much water in the path ahead of him and Horace knew he'd be lucky to make it through on what he could chew out of the plants he encountered. Lazarus would die from thirst in a few days. It was probably for the best, he told himself, that he stay behind in the heated stables with the forty-odd attentive grooms and daily walks in the courtyard and bells on his bridle. Such things were comfort-making for a horse and it made

Horace smile to think that his horse was comfortable, even if he himself were not. He trod onward.

Then there was Geoffrey. Horace felt guilty when he thought of Geoffrey. The lad was, after all, just a boy, more than a few years younger than Horace himself. He stopped then and took out the painting and looked at it, tears already wet in his eyes to protect his soft tissues from the blaring sun and harsh wind, and through that blur of self-protective excretion the figures looked distorted and changed. He rubbed his eyes on his shirt sleeve, but the impression didn't go away— the portrait was different than it had been before. Geoffrey wore a golden crown now and an even wider and more foolish grin, and Lazarus's mane was braided with red ribbons and golden thread, but it was the armor that gave Horace pause, and that was only because it had completely disappeared. And as if that weren't enough, Horace realized with preternatural dread that the legend carved into the frame had rearranged itself and now said, "Destiny and time." Impossible. He touched the carved letters but they seemed no less real, no less carved, than they had before. He had no idea what they even meant, so he put the miniature back in his pocket and plodded on. The gray line on the horizon rose as the hours wore on and became a wall and a parapet and a fortress gate with a drawbridge, but mostly it was a wall that stretched in both directions as far as Horace could see.

And then, on the seventh day of the seventh week since he left the service of the Knight of the Red Valley and began walking east towards the sun, Horace came to the gate at end of the world, the kingdom of Prester John. The city was deserted.

CHAPTER EIGHT

"Hello!" Horace yelled. He banged on the heavy wooden gate with his fist. "Hello, is anyone there!" A vulture shrieked. Horace backed up a few feet, found a rock, and chucked it at the wooden gate, but there was no reply. He walked along the wall for an hour or so, but there were no weak or low places, no forgotten ladders, no fragments of rope, and since the wall stretched on forever, there was no walking around it. A dreadful feeling churned in the pit of his stomach. He had come all this way for nothing. There was no Prester John, if there even had been any Prester John at all. Or maybe his kingdom was five thousand miles away; who knew how far the wall stretched or what he might encounter along it. Horace sat down and cried in earnest with his back to the gate and the sun looming large above his head, and he cried for the rest of the day until he fell asleep in the dust of the road and his own sorry hopelessness.

"Horace?"

Horace woke with a start the next morning. He had been dreaming that he was feasting in the hall of the World's Most Beautiful Palace under the comfortable supposition that he had died. He was much dismayed to discover he was still alive.

"Horace?" A weird little man, perhaps an inch or so taller than Horace, stooped beside him in a blue velvet robe. He wore a tonged hat on his head of the same blue wool as his garment and leaned on a wooden walking stick. When Horace stirred the man poked him with it.

"What?" Horace sat bolt upright, made a grab for the end of the stick that poked him, as any knight worth his salt would do, and shoved it against the man, who reeled around, twisted the weapon away from Horace with a grace that surprised the knight, and made Horace give it over. Then he whacked Horace on the head. "Ouch! What did you do that for?"

"Aren't you Horace of the Knights of Stupid King Mark?" the man said, tapping the walking end of the stick in the dust between them.

"I suppose I am," Horace stood, and rubbed his head, and tried hard not to make a nasty face.

The monk grunted. "Well, are you or aren't you?"

"I've not been called that," Horace said. "I mean to say, it's not my banner, I mean, no herald would assign it to my coat of arms, if I had one." He realized he was babbling then, and held his hand out for the man to shake and shoved the other one in his pocket. "I mean to say that I am Horace, and I come from Angleterre, which is the Kingdom of Stupid King Mark, but since I haven't received my arms from him, I'm not sure, I mean legally, if I really am a knight."

The monk laughed. "That's the most I've heard you say throughout this entire journey."

Horace's woolly eyebrows knitted into their furrow. "Wait, how do you know my name? And what do you mean 'heard me say'?" Then he took a breath and said, "Are you Prester John?"

"At your service!" The monk bowed against his gnarled, tongued walking stick. "Time enough remains to discuss the rest of it. Come inside and have a bath and some breakfast." Horace noticed then, for the first time, that the man wore the long chain belt of the monastic houses and a collection of keys dangled from it, at least three or four attached to every link in the chain. He sorted through them now, counting them off like the beads of the rosary, until he found the one that opened the gate. When he pushed the gate open, Horace saw beyond him, through the courtyard, past the immense gleaming buildings of the keep, to another wall, a small, more humble wall of squat red brick. Beyond that, only the deep blue sky.

"Is this really the end of the world?" he said.

"Don't know." Prester John shrugged. "Maybe it's the beginning."

The monk led Horace down the cobblestone road to an important and official-looking building at the center of the city, and as they walked, Horace was struck by the eerie peace and silence of the place. "Where is everyone?" he asked once they reached the top of the gleaming marble steps and turned back to look down on the city buildings around them.

"Gone, gone." Prester John waved his hand in the air if he couldn't be bothered by it. "Years ago, scattered to the four corners of the earth." He fanned out his fingers to show how they all disappeared, poof, like magic. Then he turned, hiked up his long blue robe, and rapped three times on an impressive oak door with the tongue of his knobby staff. Horace followed him into a very large, very dark room. High above them light flooded through arched windows and fell on the opposite wall, also high above them, too far above to be of any use to anyone on the floor. Then Prester John struck a match, lit a few of the lamps nailed to the walls here and there, and the room flooded with light. It was a throne room and everything in it appeared to have been molded of solid gold. "Don't be so star struck," the monk said. "It isn't mine." Horace took a bold step towards the throne, reached out to stroke the fine red velvet pillow in its lap, and the monk rapped him on the head with his staff. "It isn't for you either, boy."

"Yes sir." Horace followed Prester John, a bit more cautious about what he touched, through a maze of council chambers, ball rooms, art galleries— there were collections stacked everywhere, but the galleries held the strangest and most remarkable pieces: all the art of the past was collected there, even art Horace had seen sold from the tinker's cart for half a quisling, but then there were things Horace thought must represent the art of the future as well: paintings and sculptures Horace could hardly make into sense. Some seemed to represent objects that hadn't been invented yet, while others depicted abstractions like bliss or time, and these troubled Horace— but then they reached the monk's modest kitchen, an abrupt wooden table and three stick-figure chairs, a fresh loaf of bread cooling in the window and some cheese sweating on the board. The monk offered him a seat, and half the loaf of bread, and Horace was grateful to accept both.

"Do you know why you are here?" the monk said, after Horace chewed and swallowed his first bite of lunch and had a chance to drink from the cup of water he poured for them to share. It seemed like an odd question to Horace. He was used to men like the Red Knight who acted with distinct and often formal purpose laid out and trumpeted by decrees and didn't dance around things. He liked Prester John. "I'm on a quest, sir, to reverse a spell that has been cast on the princess of my country, to prevent a war." He added the last bit, about the war, in the hope that the monk would take him seriously, "and I've been given some hope that you might help me. That is, no one else knows what to do."

The ancient monk chewed thoughtfully on his sandwich for a moment, then took a long drought from their shared cup and set it back down between them. "Is that so?" was all he said. He looked terribly amused. "And you're sure the war hasn't started already?"

"No sir." Horace fiddled with a potato that sat like a lump on the top of a basket of knotty potatoes on the end of the table, the eyes all staring at him. "I was told you could help me with that as well."

"And the little portrait in your pocket, I suppose you want me to fix that too?"

"If you can, sir," Horace said, clearly embarrassed now. "I mean, if it isn't too much trouble."

"Of course not, lad. What else have I got to attend to?" The monk laughed at his own joke, but then he reached for his staff and held his hand out, palm open, to Horace. "Give it here."

Horace reached into his breast-coat pocket, pulled out the little portrait, and placed it in the monk's palm. Geoffrey and Lazarus stared blankly from the canvas; the spark of life present so sharply at first now looked faded in their eyes. "We haven't got much time," the monk said, clipping the little painting to the chain around his waist so that it dangled with the keys when he stood. Geoffrey and Lazarus waved at Horace between the folds of robe and keys. "First things first. Let's see what the present situation is with your princess, and whether there is any point in trying to resolve it."

"Thank you sir." Horace pushed back from the table when the monk did and followed him out of the kitchen, up a curling flight of stairs, and into a high tower that looked, from the base of it, to rise as high as the sky. It should take days to climb to the top, but time passed in its usual manner and the two of them reached the alchemist's library, for that was exactly what the room at the top of the tower was, before sunset. The old monk flung the door open and bits of paper, like flutter-bys— butterflies were called flutter-bys before the centuries switched the letters around— flittered out the door and into the high, thin air. Horace felt dizzy watching as they spiraled down, words and numbers spinning into an ink and parchment-colored blur. Prester John went directly to the collection of instruments stacked and packed away neatly in wooden boxes on the table.

"Hold this." Prester John thrust a box of glass vials against Horace's chest. Silver and copper spiders chittered away from the light and into the deep recesses of the stack of Bunsen burners, test tubes, and wide-bottomed beakers while the monk cleared a space on the table. A strange carving appeared on the face of the wood. It ranged all over from continents to mountain chains to endless stretches of squat brick wall, and as Horace moved forward for a closer look he saw the borders and the continents shift and change until they dissolved beneath the carving sea. "It's a map of the world through time," Prester John mumbled. "Wait a minute and the land will rise again." As if on cue, the mouth of a volcano broke through the wooden table and began spewing forth hot lava which quickly hardened into earth. The monk ignored it. "Here!" he said, and plunked a marble down on the center of the table, which had been a violent eruption only seconds before, but now settled into a stately, massive continent.

Horace reached out to pick the marble up, and Prester John batted his hand away. It was just a cat's eye marble, the kind with the color swirled through the center, and Horace, who had never seen a marble before and had no idea how to shoot a bogey, began to think the monk was pulling his leg. The continent on which the marble rested shook and broke apart and the glass sphere rolled into a crevice between the two emerging land masses. "Ask it to show you your kingdom," Prester John said. "Ask it nicely."

Horace, having grown up sleeping on the floor of the great hall in the manor of the Red Knight, and having had no more knowledge of etiquette than a demon snake, did his best to mimic the courtly manners he observed in the World's Most Beautiful Palace, but as these were dripping with sarcasm when correctly employed, they weren't really mannerly at all. He squared his shoulders, made a deep, scraping bow, and said, in his most formal and serious voice, "Oh great and noble orb of glass, please show me the condition of Angleterre."

Nothing happened. Prester John nudged the marble and it rolled a few inches along the San Andreas Fault and stopped. He looked at Horace as if to say try again, and Horace cleared his throat and bowed even lower. "Mighty and wise glass of ages, please let me see what has become of the princess and the war ..."

"No, no, no." Prester John shoved him aside. "You've got to really mean it. Dig deep! And… give the marble more specifics. What's your princess's name, for example?" Horace shifted about uncomfortably. "You don't know?" The monk put his hand on his table to steady himself but the laughter would not be staunched. He dissolved into a fit of coughing. "No matter," Prester John said, once recovered. "We'll ask the speculum. And really, lad, don't be so melodramatic about it. It's just a marble."

Horace smiled weakly and said, "Please speculum, if you can, show us the name of Stupid King Mark's daughter." For a moment it seemed nothing would happen, for all the continents breaking apart and colliding beneath the great glass marble, but then the stripe of color in the middle dissolved into a mist. From the mist a word appeared. Angelica.

"Angelica. My, that is a pretty name. Ask it to show us what Angelica's doing, at this very moment." Horace asked the marble, in the same respectful and plain manner as before to show them Angelica, and after a few dizzy seconds of whirling color at its center an image appeared. Prester John and Horace leaned in closer, and as the image clarified, the sound of laughter filled the room, hundreds of bells ringing on the toss of a horse's mane. "Well done lad," whispered Prester John, and in that instant they were transported through time and space to the throne room of the king.

The room was filled with people. Fat and lazy Stupid King Mark sat dozing on his throne, while Angelica stood, her arms folded across her chest defiantly, staring down a group of courtiers and stamping her tiny, slippered foot. "I won't marry that Duke and that's that. Let there be a war, what do I care? Preventing war is your job. Why can't you do your jobs right?" Then she turned on her pretty, slippered heel, reams of silk fluttering behind her, and she plunked down on the chair beside her father with a look of utter disdain. She was, despite the sour puss, the most beautiful woman Horace had ever seen. More beautiful even than Constance, the woman with hair like the sun.

"Devil, isn't she." Prester John poked at one of the courtiers, the gaudy jewel-encrusted chain draped over his shoulders, and said, "This must be the king's council." Horace tried to stop him, but the monk shook him off. "Don't be daft, lad. They can't see us. We aren't really here, you know."

Horace went to the window and looked out towards the border the kingdom shared with Loraine. Black smoke in scattered clouds rose on the horizon, a sure sign of a military encampment. "I think the Duke will attack any day now, unless the princess accepts his hand." A man in a black velvet doublet and a stiff lace ruff turned towards the window as if he thought he heard something, looked confused, and turned away.

"Very little time left," said the monk. He climbed the stairs at the foot of the throne and stood to the right of Stupid King Mark, looking down on the faces in the room, the wrinkles on each forehead and at the corner of every eye. "But just enough to make it worth trying for." He poked the King's belly with the business end of his staff. "Too bad this one is so useless. Terrible burden for a young girl, the running of a country." Horace, who after all was a knight, or had been before he lost his armor and his squire and horse, said nothing out of fealty to Stupid King Mark. Instead he turned his attention to the princess, who was shooting daggers at everyone in the room with her eyes. Looking at her made him weak with something he couldn't comprehend. It was like hunger, but higher up in his chest. Maybe it was love.

CHAPTER NINE

"That's enough for our purpose," Prester John said. He snapped his fingers and the illusion vanished. They were, as they had always been, in the alchemist's library at the top of the tower, the wind whistling in their ears, the princess's laughter fading away in echoes like ripples on the surface of a lake. Prester John opened a book and made several quick notes in a ledger: "Narcissistic Personality Disorder," he wrote across the top of the page and closed the book.

"Well, what do we do now?" Horace slumped against the wall, silver spider webs rubbing off against his head. "I mean, it all looks so hopeless."

"Rubbish, lad! Nothing is hopeless. Come and see." Prester John beckoned him towards the far window and Horace obliged, limping sullen across the room, because, you must remember, Horace was a teenager, and now he was in love. The monk pulled back a heavy velvet curtain with much aplomb and sunlight flooded the room, making the books and cauldrons and Bunsen burners sparkle with life. In the distance, from their vantage point high above the kingdom of Prester John, Horace could see the eastern wall. It stretched into infinity from the North Pole to the South. Prester John pointed at a gate that seemed to have been built more or less in the exact center of the wall, a squat, humble little wrought iron square with a simple wooden handle. "What do you think lies on the far side of that gate?" the monk said.

"The end of the world, I suppose," Horace said, and shrugged. He looked over his shoulder at the marble on the table. He wanted, more than anything, to go back to the throne room to be near Angelica. Sweetness hung in the air about her like perfume, despite her sour attitude, and to Horace that sweetness was like nectar to a bee. He imagined it was so for any man that happened to be near her, and a pang of jealousy struck his heart.

"Focus, lad." Prester John shook him by the shoulder. "You're closer to the end of your quest than you think."

"Is that another one of your riddles?"

Prester John whacked Horace with the business end of his staff. Then the monk leaned against the wall and turned a metal crank near the window, a creaking pulley gear that wound around a cable so thin it might be made of spider web. A black harness appeared in the distance and soon it came creaking through the window as the monk turned the crank. "Strap in," he said, hiking up his robe to step into the leather harness, holding a similarly connected apparatus out for Horace. Once he was satisfied that they were both reasonably secure, he stepped onto the ledge of the window, his robes billowing in the wind. "Let's go," he said.

"You are insane!" Horace was just about to shout: "There is no way I am climbing through that window," but Prester John grabbed him by his collar, and as he was already strapped into the harness, he had little choice but to go. In minutes they reached the squat brick wall and Horace, cursing worse than Geoffrey, landed flat on his face in the sand. There was a staff, just like the one he'd left behind in the tower, leaning against the low brick wall, and once he'd climbed free of his harness, the monk took up the staff and beat Horace with it. "Stand up and clean yourself off, stupid boy. You're about to meet your maker."

Just then, as if it listened to their conversation, the latch unlatched itself and the wrought iron gate, grown green with old vines, swung itself open, creaking. Horace stared with equal parts wonder and apprehension through the space cleared by the absence of the door. Every tree and flower ever created turned toward the open gate and away from the rising sun, and a hush fell over the garden otherwise humming with life. "Go on then." Prester John poked Horace in the back with the root of his staff.

"Aren't you coming too?"

"Can't. It's not my quest." Horace nodded, considering this, and turned again towards the ancient path through the impossible garden. "When you return, I'll be here waiting for you." Then Horace heard the gate close, and the clatter of the lock clicking into place filled him with dread. He wanted to run back, fling it open, and resign from the quest on the spot. Instead, he stuffed his hands in the pockets of his dung peddler's pants. He would have started down the path through the garden, but a loud banging came from the far side of the gate. Horace ran back, tugged on the gate until it swung open, and Prester John stood there holding out a small scroll in a leather case, so small that it fit squarely in the old man's palm. He thrust it towards Horace and said, "Here, I forgot to give you this."

"Is that all?" Horace held the scroll between his thumb and forefinger. All in all, the scroll in its case was no bigger than a tube of lipstick. "What is it?"

"Carry it with you, and when the time comes that you need it, you'll know." The monk turned on his heel to go, and Horace shouted after him, "Hey! What kind of game is this?" but the monk only waved his hand and kept walking.

Horace gave Prester John the side eye, and the old monk responded by pushing closed the gate.

Then there was nothing else to do but walk forward. When the gate first opened, and Horace and Prester John's faces first appeared there framed in wrought iron and vines, all the plants and flowers of the garden turned towards them in shocked silence, the flutter-bys pausing to hover mid flutter. They, all of them, turned away now, mystified by the sudden reappearance of a man among them. A ripple of worried questions ran through the flower beds and orchids as the insects hopped and fluttered and frittered away, but to Horace it looked like the wind whispering through grasses, each plant asking her neighbor where the man had come from and what on earth he could want. Plants, you see, all take the feminine pronoun. Whether or not they are all female is another matter entirely. Nevertheless, each flower turned to her sister and whispered, "What can he want?" then trembled and hid her face as Horace approached.

And so Horace walked, through weeks and months and years, and he encountered not one being that asked if she could help him find his way. His stomach grumbled and his body ached with exhaustion, but still he walked, sometimes wondering in passing when he would need to stop to eat or sleep, but no urges spurred him to slow his gate and many years passed before he was aware of the passage of time. Then one day— and here day is meant in the sense of a period of time, for if the sun rose and set, Horace was not aware of it; in fact the sun, unyielding and brutal, hovered exactly in its apex high above him, trying to turn him back— then one day he came to the center of the garden. No special ceremonial object marked the place. It just seemed to Horace that if he took another step forward, he would finally surpass the sun and move forward with it at his back, burning down on his neck, and it was more out of dread of that possibility than any other reason that drove Horace to stop walking and, for the first time in eons, sit down to rest.

A bed of red tulips waited for him, so soft it looked like the feather pallet he slept on in the high tower room of the Most Beautiful Palace in the World. He settled down into it, leaning back on his folded hands, watched the clouds above him, and thought about their funny shapes. One looked like the miniature portrait he'd given Prester John, and another looked like the clubbed staff the man used to whack him. None of the clouds moved. They hovered static above him with the cruel, unwavering sun. Then Horace noticed something truly strange: all the flowers in the field had turned toward him, despite the direction from which their attention originated. He could see their faces, and what's more they seemed to be breathing with him; when his chest rose, so did each flower, shrub, bush, scrub and tree, until Horace developed the distinct impression that they were all one organism that covered the entire face of the Earth. And that was when he first heard them singing.

It is a little known fact that plants (all plants from your mother's most exalted hydrangea bush on down to the lowliest Boston bug weed) sing, and sing constantly. It is as natural and essential to their function as talking or consuming overpriced products from overseas factories is to ours. They care very little what they sing, and most of it is a garbled cacophony of discordant notes, patches of songs picked up from passing worms, and the echo of car horns across millenniums, but on occasion they come together and hum the same note in unison, and it was one of these occasions that Horace happened to witness from his bed of tulips at the center of the garden at the end of the world. He thought his heart might explode from the loveliness of it. The flowers leaned towards him, each one humming, and then it occurred to him that they were tuning up, the way an orchestra hums and groans together as it tunes itself to the first oboe. And then Horace remembered the scroll.

He had it in the back pocket of his pants. He reached down now, oh so lazily as it had been, by this point, another hundred years or so since he last moved his hand, and extracted the tiny scroll in its tight leather case, pulled it from the confines of its tiny leather keepings, and unrolled it, half unsure where it had come from (hundreds of years had passed since he'd received it) and only the vague impression left that the scroll was some sort of instruction from some sort of king. All the while the humming of the flowers intensified; Horace felt their voices shaking in the back of his throat and in the pit of his stomach; his hands even shook as he unrolled the scroll, but instead of instructions written on the face of the brown foxing ancient paper, he found a song. *The Song of Horace.*

Horace knew what to do, just as Prester John said he would, although it was ages since they'd spoken and Prester John was only a vague notion of a memory by then. Horace knew exactly what to do, and moreover, he couldn't stop himself from doing it. The humming of the flowers flooded his cardiac cavity and the song burst forth, in perfect pitch, directly from his immense heart, more pure and more perfect than even the songs the birds sang, as if Horace's natural condition, or by extension, the natural condition of humanity, was melodic, tonal, and rhythmic; it was as if his body were an instrument comprised entirely of strings. And so Horace went on singing, and he may have sung until the end of time, but he came to the end of the first movement, and looked up, and there happened to be a person standing where none had stood before.

The person, it was hard to tell if it was a man or a woman, wore a long white tunic, although white is an imprecise word for the color of the tunic; there is no word in our language to describe its color, but many readers would find "blank" an acceptable substitute. If the person's tunic was blank, as was the person's hair, the eyes that shone in the center of the face, also of a hue that has no name in English, were a conglomerate of all colors, as if one were looking at each color simultaneously and seeing them all rather than one murky pool of nothing, which is to say that the person's eyes were the color of everything. These orbs of everything regarded Horace now with a mixture of intimidation and unflinching acceptance, as if waiting for Horace to say something very important. Horace stammered, a stray note popped out of his mouth and floated in the air between them, and then Horace had the notion that he should bow. He hopped to his feet and grasped himself at the waist and made ready to double over as low as possible, but mercifully, as Horace was as clumsy as he had been thousands of years before in the hall of the Red Knight, the person made a gesture to put a stop to it and Horace stumbled back and fell into the grass where the flowers folded around him in a supportive embrace. "Tell me," the person said, "why you are here."

"Please sir, madam… sir," Horace mumbled, but the person took no notice of his clumsiness, "please, I come from a kingdom where a terrible tragedy has befallen the princess…" and then a strange thought occurred to Horace, "at least, there was a tragedy, but that was so long ago now, I don't know what has become of any of them." He looked down at his shoes, twisting nervously in the dirt, afraid to meet the person's gaze. "I mean, surely the war ended long ago and none of this matters now…"

The person smiled kindly, but something in his or her eyes suggested that he or she was laughing at him. "You are a knight, are you not?" he or she said, after several days passed in silence.

"I was a knight, before I lost my armor, and my squire, and my horse," Horace said, but the figure cut him off.

"A courageous heart makes a knight," he or she said, "not the things that come along with knighthood. Kneel." Horace obliged him or her, dropping to his knee as if Stupid King Mark himself commanded it. The person put his or her hand on Horace's shoulder. "Your quest," he or she said, "is valid, and at last you have come to the knowledge that you seek, and it is this: there is no such thing as a curse. Your princess believes she is cursed, and so she appears to be. Return, wait for the princess fall in love with you, and she will forget her selfishness and all will be as it should be."

Horace stared up at the person with his or her hand on his shoulder, his face almost as blank as his or her gown, but his mind raced with questions. After a day or two of respectful silence, the person said, "You may ask me what you wish to ask," but Horace could think of nothing beyond the obvious question of how to go about getting a princess to fall in love with him, since she had never seen him, and because he was the dung peddler's son, and on account of how he was so very, very short, but the person answered him before Horace opened his mouth to speak.

"Go home." And with that, he or she vanished, leaving nothing behind save his or her words bobbing and chiming on the wind.

Horace, who had come all this way across deserts and impossible odds, through centuries and in and out of time, shoved his hands in his pockets. It looked like the end of the quest was its beginning. That was natural enough, he supposed. He was a knight, or wanted to be one. It wasn't as if he didn't expect another quest to come his way eventually. And so Horace, after thousands of years at the center of the garden, simply got to his feet and went home. All the flowers turned to watch, each one wondering when and where they would see him again. The flowers in the garden at the end of the world, as blessedly suspended in time as we are here when we come together in this story, know that they can always see you again, the next time around. It is all anyone has to look forward to.

I cannot say with certainty that Horace understood this when he started walking out of the garden, but I can say that he left his song behind, where it waits for the next time he needs it.

CHAPTER TEN

Prester John stood waiting for him on the far side of the gate. Horace didn't recognize him at first, barely remembered him, but then he heard himself saying, "I hope you didn't stand here waiting the whole time." As he pulled the gate closed and crossed through the threshold all that time vanished, forgotten, leaving only the impressions of a dream.

"Twelve minutes?" Prester John checked the clock dangling from his belt. He picked up his staff and turned to walk back towards his castle. He didn't even ask how Horace had been.

"But I was in there…" Horace hurried after the old monk, "for what felt like forever…" Horace had the uncomfortable feeling one has when waking from a dream that one has been somewhere extraordinary but can't quite remember where. "I just thought I'd come out and everything would be thousands of years ago."

"Time is relative. And so, incidentally, is space. Your friends are waiting." He banged his staff on the cobblestone walk for emphasis and waved it at the high tower, so high above them it was hidden in the clouds.

"My friends?" Horace squinted, but it didn't make the tower window any easier to see.

Prester John poked Horace in the chest with the staff, ex-

97

asperated. "Your friends, your friends. The horse and the young man, what did you call them? Lizard? Garth? The ones in the portrait." He stopped then, in mid-stride, reached into his robe, and pulled out a long spyglass exactly like the ones big game hunters use on safari. The instrument telescoped as he pulled it from his robe, and when he handed it to Horace, it was at least as long as his staff. "See for yourself."

Sure enough, there in the window were Lazarus, more belled and bow-tied than ever, and Geoffrey, a bit more fat and florid than Horace remembered and much more sullen and slow than he should be. "How'd you do that?"

"You can thank the alchemist later." Prester John folded the telescope back into the pocket of his robe and on they walked. They walked in silence until they came to the first balustrade of the castle keep, and then Prester John stopped Horace at the foot of the stairs and said, "Now that you've been out of the garden longer than you were in it," and what a marvelously odd statement that was, from Horace's point of view, "do you remember what it said to you? About your quest, I mean."

"Ummm… no, not really." And that was true. Had Horace been able to remember anything at all about the thousands and thousands of years he had lived in the garden, he would have remembered that the being who spoke to him was not a human being but something more like an earthworm. The old monk looked at him as if he were very sorry for the young man, and Horace smiled and shrugged. "You know what? I think I'll remember when I need to remember."

At least a thousand steps remained, but that was not nearly so far as the seven thousand stairs they'd already climbed, when Horace could finally make out Geoffrey at the window shouting down to them with a cross, impatient look on his face, unaware that the wind carried every word he said away from the tower and out over the garden almost as soon as it left his lips. It was another thousand steps before Horace and the monk could hear him. Once they did reach shouting distance, they heard nothing but curses and complaining "…and they were just about to make me Lord of Misrule! If you hadn't butted in with your magic spells, sucking me up into this tower all filled with horse stink, they might have made me king!"

In the small room at the top of the tower, Lazarus nuzzled through the shallow bowls and pestles and kettles and didn't see much reason to stop for the sudden reappearance of his master. Horace patted his flank, and the horse bristled, swung his enormous head Horace's way, and glared at him. Geoffrey ran right up to Horace and kicked him in the shin. When Prester John laughed, he turned to the old monk and said in the most sarcastic, beautiful palace voice he could muster, "And who are you, some magician?"

"He's the king here," said Horace.

That got Geoffrey's attention. He straightened his posture, turned a humble face towards the old monk and made a very respectful low bow. "It's a pleasure to make your acquaintance, your highness."

"Likewise." Prester John smiled at Horace, tired wrinkles in the corners of his eyes. "Now that you've got what you came for,

I suppose you'll be on your way." He reached into the pocket of his long robe, pulled out a small object, and held it out for Horace to take. It was the miniature portrait, a sumptuous rendering of one interior wall of the World's Most Beautiful Palace, a stray button on the table in the corner of the picture. The legend at the bottom had morphed again; now the message read, "We keep a part of you, always." That made Horace uneasy, but he pocketed the portrait all the same.

It took nine hours to coax Lazarus down the broken stone steps that wound around the tower in the harsh eastern wind, and another five to pick their way through the cobblestone streets towards the western wall of the monk's kingdom, or it should have taken five hours, but Geoffrey couldn't resist poking his snub nose through abandoned doorways and into forgotten shops. "What happened to all your subjects?" he asked, intermittently, rephrasing it as though it were an entirely new question each time, never quite satisfied with the answer.

"I don't know. One morning they were all gone." Prester John hobbled along and the sound of his walking stick echoed through the empty city.

"Gone? As in they decided to move on without telling you? Or as in they simply vanished?" Horace tried to catch Geoffrey's eye, but Geoffrey refused to look at Horace altogether. "You don't know where they've gone, do you?"

"I think I have a pretty good idea," the monk said, and that was all he said on the matter, despite Geoffrey's best efforts to drag more of the story out of him.

The next morning, Horace woke Geoffrey early and saddled the horse. The monk rolled over in the ragged cot that served for a bed in his monk's cell beneath the tower stairs, watched them dressing and shuffling about, and then closed his eyes and went back to sleep. He didn't even rouse himself to see them off.

"Why do you think he's so sad?" Geoffrey picked an apple from a solitary tree growing in the center of one of the cobblestone streets. "I mean, if I were the king of my own kingdom, I wouldn't have a care in the world. And I sure wouldn't sleep in a servant's hovel under the stairs."

"I think all his people passed through the gate so long ago, he can't remember now. I feel kind of sorry for him."

"He should have come with us," Geoffrey watched the portcullis shutter as it closed them out of the kingdom. "There's hundreds of people in the next palace over. Good people who know how to have fun."

"This isn't the gate I'm talking about." Horace stopped to knot the leather on Lazarus's reigns, the better to lead him. Horace still hadn't learned how to ride. "You know, it's fine by me if you want to try and go back to them. I got along just fine without you. I didn't ask Prester John to pull you out of that painting, anyway."

"Fine. Constance will be pleased." That was all they said to each other for outwards of a week as they picked their way carefully along the high mountain pass that brought them back down into the lowlands and slowly towards the crystalline palace that faced the sunset so defiantly. As they drew closer, it became very hard for Geoffrey to contain all the language that bubbled up in him, funny quips of Constance's or little memories of times he made everyone around him dissolve in envious laughter; all of Geoffrey's favorite memories of his time spent in the World's Most Beautiful Palace were of times that this or that fellow had been envious of him, so much so that as the features of the castle became clear on the horizon, he began to imagine that he could see people in the windows, waving in welcome to him. Soon he had convinced himself that they had prepared a Welcome Home feast in his honor. Horace, who didn't need to hear Geoffrey's vain imaginings to guess the source of his discomfort, was forced to plod dutifully beside Lazarus, hoping that once they reached the palace the beautiful people would at least spare Geoffrey's feelings and have some little party for him or some token to soothe his ego, but soon it became apparent to Horace, if it wasn't already apparent to Geoffrey, that the palace was empty.

Maybe it always had been. Horace didn't want Geoffrey to panic, so he kept his mouth shut about it until there was no other way but to see plainly with one's own eyes that the castle was deserted. This was how they came to stand at the palace gate, knocking on the door for no one to come and open it, for no one was exactly who heard the knocking, and so no one was exactly who came.

"Stop that, there's no one there." Horace put a hand on Geoffrey's shoulder. Geoffrey had given up pounding on the door with his fists and had now taken to banging on the wooden planks with his own head.

"They've got to be here! Where would they go?" Geoffrey

kicked the door again, so hard that tears of frustration formed in the corners of his eyes.

Lazarus nuzzled Horace's chest and Horace patted his nose and then pushed his horsey head away. "Maybe they followed Prester John's subjects through the garden gate." Geoffrey gave Horace a withering look. Lazarus nuzzled his chest again, intent on getting into his breast coat pocket, and Horace shoved him off more forcefully. "Maybe they were never here in the first place. Maybe we only believed they were here, and they were only figments of our imagination."

"If they were figments of our imagination, why wouldn't they still be here? We're here to imagine them, aren't we?" Lazarus, who apparently felt he had been ignored for much of the journey and would have his opinion known now, whinnied and butted his head against Horace's chest and knocked the wind out of him. Horace wheezed and puffed, flat on his back, and the tiny, empty portrait rolled out of his pocket and clattered on the ground beside him. Geoffrey grabbed for it, but Horace held him off with one arm as he sat up, still fighting for his breath. Together the two of them examined the picture. Everything was just as it had been before, the sumptuous wall delicately painted and staring back at them, the image devoid of human form… but something had changed. In the right hand corner of the frame, where Horace had last seen one of Geoffrey's buttons resting on the bedside table, there was, where the button had been, now the whisper of a hand reaching out to take something from the table. The legend carved into the frame had changed as well. "Something to remember you by," was what it said.

"They're in the portrait?!" Geoffrey screamed. He turned and shoved Horace, who almost doubled over again. "We were in the portrait! Why didn't you leave us there?!"

"It's a curse," Horace almost said, but something in the back of his mind stopped him. He had the strangest memory, a ghost of a dream intruding on his waking life, of an earthworm telling him there was no such thing as a curse, despite all appearances to the contrary. He took a deep breath. "Go there, then. Go in after them." He shoved the portrait into Geoffrey's hands. "What's stopping you?"

Geoffrey held the painting in the palm of his hand. "It's... just paint."

"Yeah, so?" Horace pinched Geoffrey's forearm. "You're just flesh and blood."

"I don't know what you're talking about."

Geoffrey shoved the painting in his pocket and got up to give the gate another angry kick.

"I mean, if you believe you were in the portrait before, and you actually were in the portrait before, I think you could believe yourself right back into it, if you really want in it that bad. The fact that you're here at all tells me you're exactly where you want to be."

Geoffrey pounded on the gate because he was exactly where he wanted to be, except that all the sycophantic courtiers had gone and there was no one to welcome him with a feast and a tournament. It was nightfall before he gave up. "Maybe if we walk around to the front gate, where the lake is, they'll see us and come out." And so they did.

The World's Most Beautiful Palace didn't have the advantage of straddling the fault line between the tangible and the unknown, so there was no immense wall stretching across the horizon. They picked their way around the perimeter in less than a day. But something was different about Geoffrey, and at times the difference was close to intolerable. Horace looked at him once or twice, certain to catch him crying. "Stupid horse, why can't you go any faster," he said at one point when Lazarus stopped to drink from a stream of water sluicing down the castle wall and off the grate of some high turret. His sighs were louder than Lazarus's intermittent grunts of frustration. "If only I knew why they all left," Geoffrey mumbled, one of several hundred things he said under his breath that afternoon. "If I only I knew why."

By the time they reached the world's deepest lake they were exhausted. Horace made a camp in the shadow of the upended swan boat that still sat half buried in sand, the only evidence they could find that anyone had ever been there at all.

Night fell, and the small fire Horace built cast eerie shadows on the castle, so that it appeared to Geoffrey the feasting had begun again, and so it appeared to Horace the castle burned at the heart of the flames, and so it appeared to Lazarus the castle would shake loose of its foundation and go spinning off into space for reasons beyond the scope of this narrative. The illusion made Geoffrey even more upset, and he tore his shirt and screamed at the lake, "Hey lizard! Hey you big prehistoric beast! Did you eat

Constance?" Horace ran to the shore and clapped his hand over Geoffrey's mouth and tried to drag him back to the safety of the swan's one exposed wing, but Geoffrey wanted none of it and took a swing at his knight. Horace ducked, which only made Geoffrey swing harder, and soon they were rolling in the sand, slapping and kicking one another, trying to gain the upper hand. Lazarus watched them, chewing some sea grass without much emotion.

When Geoffrey finally gave in, Horace stood up and brushed the dirt from his clothes, which by this time had regressed to the beggar's rags he wore before even entering the Red Knight's service, so that after all his daring deeds and shows of honorable virtue, he looked just like the son of a dung peddler. "Look!" Horace pointed at the empty crystal castle behind them.

"Look at your palace. You want to be king there? Fine, alright, you're king!" He took a stray laurel branch from the mass of vines decorating the swan's broken back and placed it on Geoffrey's head for a crown.

Geoffrey, propped in the dirt with his hands, threw the laurel branch back at him. "Stop treating me like a child!" He curled up in a ball in the sand there, and whether he was sleeping or not, Horace didn't know. He didn't make a sound for the rest of the night.

The sun rose red on a blue morning, and the three awoke to a refreshing fog burning off the surface of the lake.

"Let's get on with it," Geoffrey said. He heaved his body against the swan boat and tried to push it on its side.

"I'm not sure that swan will help us," Horace said, but he went to Geoffrey's side and helped him right the boat anyway. As sand sloughed off the carcass, a skeleton of wood and iron junctions emerged beneath the feather and tulle façade.

Geoffrey yanked off a strip of cloth and the swan's shoulder and wing pulled away to reveal a functional, if modest, dingy beneath. "It's just a boat," he sighed. Then he sank down into the ground beside it, crossed his arms over his legs, and stared off into the distance.

Horace, who knew all along it was just a boat, went on stripping the fabric away, and soon there was a pile of bird feathers, tulle, and cotton swathing frothing at his feet. "Snap out of it," he said when Geoffrey sighed aloud for the fifteenth time. "You'll be home again soon."

"That's what I'm afraid of." Once the boat was repaired, and half afloat in the water, and Horace and Lazarus were loaded starboard side, Horace held his hand out to Geoffrey and tried to help him in. Geoffrey looked back at the castle, then into the boat, then back at the castle again. "I don't want to go home."

"Why? What's keeping you?"

"I don't know. This is the only place I've ever felt wanted."

Geoffrey climbed into the boat reluctantly. "You'll feel that way again," Horace said as he pushed away from the shore. The little boat noised its way out into the black water, the surface of the lake as still as glass.

107

CHAPTER ELEVEN

The Deepest Lake in the World is not only the deepest lake in the world; several studies suggest it is also the saddest. That is to say that people report feeling sadder in the vicinity of the Deepest Lake in the World than they do in any other spot on the earth's surface. All things being equal, Geoffrey, having lost his entire kingdom just as swiftly and mysteriously as Prester John, had more cause for being sad when they first embarked on their voyage home than anyone ever to float across the world's deepest lake, and so became the saddest boy in history. He insisted on leaning over the side of the boat and dragging his fingers in the black, stagnant water and neither Horace's pleas nor Lazarus's snorts of frustration could dissuade him. And it was his great sadness, in the end, that attracted the monster.

They were halfway across the lake before the sun drooped and stained the western sky a deep bruised purple. In fact, had they crossed the lake at any other point in the day, Geoffrey may not have fallen into such terrible melancholia as to attract the primitive beast, but at precisely half-past six, with the chancellery bells still ringing, Geoffrey happened to look up from his reflection on the dark surface of the water and saw the setting sun reflecting back from the castle, which seemed aglow with its own interior fire in the sunlight, very much the way a vain person's eyes sparkle in the mirror, and these events colluded to convince Geoffrey that he'd been fooled again.

"They've lit the fires!" he shouted, and jumped to his feet, rocking the small boat so much that Lazarus reared back and nearly upended them. "They've started the dancing! I can hear the music…" and then he stopped, craned his neck towards the castle, and for once he wanted everyone else to hush. "Don't you hear it? The pipes and the fiddles?" Horace reached out to try and yank him back, but it was too late; Geoffrey was already pacing back and forth on the ship's bow. "I smell roast swan! Capers and trout! And bread baking! Horace, we have to go back!" Geoffrey jumped up and down on the edge of the boat now, rocking the vessel back and forth, unconcerned by the water seeping over the edge and up through the floorboards. Horace yanked him back by the shirt collar and Geoffrey whirled around and decked Horace square on the jaw. "You're jealous!" he shouted, though the wind had picked up around them and made his words hard to hear. "You can't be king, so I can't either, is that it? Constance doesn't love you, she loves me!"

"Who said anything about her?" Clearly, Geoffrey was not in the mood to listen to reason.

"You did, you cowardly liar! Well, we'll see who's king and who's squire!" Geoffrey rustled out of his coat and flung it on the soggy floorboards of the boat. "We'll see who's just the son of a dung peddler!"

"Geoffrey!" Horace screamed, but by the time the scream left his lips, it was too late. Horace watched in horror as Geoffrey squared up on the edge of the boat, arched his body, dove into the water, and started to swim for shore. He'd barely uttered the phrase "COME BACK" when he saw the tail fin, enormous as the backdraft of a 747, flip out of the water. An open mouth, ancient, rotting teeth dripping with black water and kelp, parted, and Geoffrey disappeared under the waves. Until the end of his life Horace swore that in that one second when he looked into the eye of the prehistoric beast, he saw Constance looking back at him, and she was laughing.

Once it was all over the lake fell preternaturally silent. Horace sat, dumbstruck, for a minute or more; in truth, he was too afraid to move for fear that any change in the lake's current would call the monster's attention to the surface once again. But the moment passed, and Horace found himself in the next moment, still alone, but blessedly still equipped with a functional paddle and a mostly dry boat bottom, and if those were his only advantages in the situation, at least he was already halfway across the lake. "Don't you jump overboard on me, too," he said to Lazarus. Lazarus laid his head on the edge of the dingy and stared at the spot where Geoffrey disappeared. "I know." Horace sighed and folded Geoffrey's jacket up and tucked it into his vest. "But we can't do anything about it now. We'll just have to get on with it, won't we?" Lazarus snorted. There was nothing else to say. They reached the western shore and the creature did not resurface, and after half an hour more they knew it was time to go on.

They trudged through the Desert of Unfathomable Nightmares without incident and soon Horace and Lazarus stood at the edge of the Forbidden Forest, staring into the yard of Geoffrey's family farm under the shade cast by the strange oak tree. "I don't know how I'm going to tell his aunt," Horace said. Lazarus put his head on Horace's shoulder, his long black eyelashes masking the human look in his eyes. "I guess the best way is to just get it over with." Lazarus nudged him forward with his nose. "Ok, ok, I'm going." It was not the homecoming he expected, dressed in rags and returning only with a handful of wild stories about faraway castles and a half-remembered bit of common sense advice from a being that he grew increasingly certain was an earthworm. Well, there was no help for it. He took a step, crossing over the threshold from desert to forest that was so easily traceable at that moment in our planet's evolution, and with every step he took through the forest thereafter, small purple flowers grew in the indentations left behind by his feet. Horace had returned home, a true knight.

Geoffrey's family was just sitting down to supper, a thick weasel stew, when Horace knocked on the squat door of their low forest hovel. His aunt barely recognized Horace when she opened the door, such a man he had become. In fact, she said, "There's a MAN at the door!" and slammed it in his face.

Geoffrey's uncle came to the door with a piece of straw in his mouth and no teeth in his head, gumming at the stem. He opened the door, stuck his face through the opening, then slammed the door shut again. "It's that knight fellow that Geoffrey went off with," Horace heard him say through the open window. He could hear furniture moving about inside and it sounded as if the elderly blacksmith was making his way back to his seat at the table, unconcerned.

"Well don't you think we should let him in?" When his aunt came to the door again, she had a dripping spoon in her hand. The otters spilled through the doorway of the cottage and wrestled on the ground at their feet. "Please excuse me sir, but I thought you were one of those mercenaries again.

Come in, come in, but leave that horse outside."

Horace tied Lazarus to a nearby tree. "My thanks," he said, and took the bowl of stew offered to him, which he ate with great appreciation.

It wasn't long before they realized that Geoffrey wasn't with him. Geoffrey's aunt fidgeted in her seat while his Uncle insisted that they let the man finish his meal before they dug in to pestering him, and Horace was loathe to begin, so his aunt filled the silence with lurid, overheard tales of atrocities committed by the mercenary soldiers of the Duke of Loraine, who had for some time menaced the inhabitants of Stupid King Mark's wood. "They say Angelica grows more and more petulant every day, and nothing will satisfy her... and worse, they say the Duke of Loraine has offered her his hand."

"Why is that worse, Mother?" Geoffrey's uncle looked over his newspaper.

"Because, you nincompoop, she refused it. She could end this misery this minute if only she'd think of someone else for a change."

Something about that struck Horace strangely, and reminded him of something the earthworm said, but it struck him in the gut, which has no language, so he couldn't piece together the meaning of it. He pushed his bowl away, covered his mouth to conceal a burp, and Geoffrey's aunt hushed immediately and stared at him. Horace looked very, very sorry.

"Where is Geoffrey..." she said, after a minute more had passed.

"Geoffrey was... Geoffrey died fighting off a prehistoric dragon. He saved my life." Horace didn't know why he said that. Even as the words came out of his mouth, he realized they were not what he had intended to say, and now that they were streaming out in long sentences, he felt powerless to stop them. "You should both be very proud of him; he was a true squire to the end." He remembered then that he had the boy's jacket, and he pulled it out of his vest so that it looked as though he had carried it, all that way, close to his heart. "I thought you might want this, ma'am." He held out the small green coat to the woman who'd made it. Geoffrey's aunt took the garment, hid her face, and sobbed.

The old blacksmith pushed his chair away from the table. "You'd better come with me, son." He put his hand on Horace's shoulder in a fatherly manner. "She'll be at that for a while." Horace pushed back from the table and followed the old man, who led him through the cottage door and into his blacksmith shop. In the back corner, under a massive tarp, something roughly the size and shape of a young man waited. The blacksmith threw the tarp back with a flourish to reveal a nearly complete set of armor made of hammered gold.

It was as beautifully crafted as any set of armor Horace had ever seen. The helmet, a proper slatnosed peak of a shape that will remind modern readers of a bullet, gleamed with fire, and Horace reached out to touch it, then pulled his fingers back as if it might really burn. "It's ok, lad. Take it; try it out. I made the thing to be used." It was magnificent; that Horace could tell just from the curve of the golden helmet, light as a paper crown. "Try it on," the blacksmith urged him, and Horace was amazed to discover that it slipped neatly into place, the runners lining up precisely with his ears. "Bend forward now," the blacksmith uncle said, and when Horace complied, he knocked on the gold bell and put his ear next to the metal face to listen to the echo made in the cavity nearly filled by Horace's head. "7 ¼ quarter," he muttered to himself. "That's not much more than Geoffrey." He made a note on his table top in scratchy charcoal pencil, then he turned toward Horace with a length of string in his hand and said, "Hold out your wrist for me." Of course Horace obliged the man, and the blacksmith tied the string around his wrist, knotted it twice, and cut the loop just shy of the second knot. "Not bad," the blacksmith said, leaving Horace to wonder exactly what it was about his wrist that was not bad, but he felt too shy and too ashamed to press the man.

Horace ran his hand over the breastplate resting on the table, tracing the outline of the coat of arms glinting in the firelight. "You are an artist, Sir."

"Too bad I'm not an alchemist," the blacksmith said. He pulled the cloth over the collection of hammered metal, and Horace noticed a significant loss of light in the room. The old man sat down on his workbench, drew a loose straw from his pocket, and chewed it thoughtfully. "Geoffrey was a good boy, a bit of a smart mouth, but he made me proud on occasion. He was like a son to Mother. We never had any of our own, you know."

"Yes sir," Horace said, mainly because he wasn't sure what else to say.

"He was a vain young man," the blacksmith continued, and he laughed and leaned his head in his hand, the straw dangling from his lips. "You know what he wanted for his coat of arms? Guess." He prodded Horace then, lightly, with the dry end of the straw. "Go ahead and guess."

"A dragon?" Horace guessed.

The blacksmith shook with laughter. "That's Geoffrey, alright. You pinned him. Not only a dragon, though. He wanted Saint George as well, and a sword piercing the great beast's heart." Then he turned his attention back to his work. "What was on your coat of arms before you lost your armor?"

Horace smiled. "I can't say it was truly my coat of arms. I inherited my armor from a knight named Lazarus, an honorable and true knight, but that was so long ago. It's strange; I can't say I remember. It seems as though it was some sort of tree…"

The blacksmith picked up the charcoal pencil again and sketched a knobby old oak tree on the table's surface, its huge branches trembling like reeds in the wind. "An ancient oak tree, that's what it was. I remember now. This belonged to Lazarus, you say?"

Horace nodded. "I wonder why he chose such an odd symbol." He tried to remember the knight's face, but Horace had lived thousands of years since then, even if the world around him had gone along at its normal pace, and everything that happened to him when he was Lazarus's squire was dimly shrouded by the cobwebs of time.

The blacksmith pressed the pencil into his hand. "Draw for me," he said, "what you would put on your own coat of arms." Horace took the pencil, but at first he wasn't sure what he should draw. No one had ever asked him that before, and it certainly never occurred to him that anyone might, as choosing one's own coat of arms was something that rarely happened, and usually only to the very wealthy and well-placed. Horace had always been penniless; he barely had claim to the kind of coat of arms most men would reward themselves with. A griffon, reared back to attack, was flat out. Saint George slaying the dragon would look just as ridiculous on his own chest as it would have looked on Geoffrey's. Horace moved the pencil a bit, just to humor Geoffrey's uncle, not really meaning to draw anything at all, but when he moved his hand aside he saw an earthworm standing on its final few segments as if it were a man. "What's that?" the old blacksmith asked.

"An earthworm?" Horace was struck then by the conviction that the earthworm seemed to be the least important creature in existence precisely because it was the most important, but again it was that gut feeling that had no language, ineffable and fleeting. "They turn the soil," he said, weakly.

"That they do," Geoffrey's uncle said and slapped the table. He plucked the straw from his mouth and chucked it in the fire, then coaxed the burning logs about until they shifted and crumbled in a shudder of sparks. "That they do. We best be back to the Misses; I'm sure she's had her cry out and turned her energies to baking by now." Horace followed him back into the cottage, stealing a last look at the outline of the suit of armor on the table. Geoffrey would have loved it. He laughed when he imagined Geoffrey, gold-plated, head thrown back in a battle cry, hacking indiscriminately at the air with a sword far too big for his body. It was a shame, really. The pie his Aunt made, however, was lovely, and, stuffed to drowsy with boysenberry and clotted cream, he fell asleep in the chair by the cottage fire and didn't even notice when they gently removed his well-worn shoes.

When he woke the next morning, Horace found a note pinned to his coat pocket, written out in heavy charcoal scrawl. It read, "Have gone to see the World's Most Beautiful Palace. Please take the pie on the table and the armor in the shop." On the kitchen table a few pieces of pie sat wrapped in butcher paper waiting to be taken along; in the courtyard Lazarus still munched from a pail of oats someone had suspended from his tether. Horace patted the horse on the flank, and Lazarus glared at him, face still in the bucket. The white cloth covering the armor flapped in a gust of wind through the blacksmith's workshop, and Horace drew back the hastily-draped cloth. Beneath it the suit of armor sparkled in the scant light still thrown off of the coals burning in the modest forge, arrayed as if the owner was expected to rise up from the table at any moment. On the breastplate the old blacksmith, by some magic Horace would never fathom, had etched the image of an earthworm into the gold.

There was, regrettably, no one there to help him dress, and as with many of the elaborate costumes of times past and times future, there is no getting into a suit of armor without at least four pairs of hands, so Horace had no choice but to pack the collection of plates, mail and shield into a loose bundle. He strapped the parcel to Lazarus's saddle bag. The small leather pouch, inadequate to so much baggage, barely concealed the armor and the toe of one shin guard protruded from under the mouth of the leather satchel, but it would travel. Horace shook the saddle to make sure nothing would fall out and then went back into the cottage to help himself to some pie. That he could carry in his stomach. He wrote a note of thanks to the couple in the discarded pie paper and looked around the cottage sadly. He would not, he imagined, see Geoffrey's family again.

The road through the Forbidden Forest had widened by several feet since Horace last followed the Knight Lazarus along it, and from the looks of things, precious little had changed for the other knights engaged in the King's quest. No more than ten minutes into the thicket, Horace and Lazarus came upon the body of a man killed in battle, blue in the lips but otherwise looking like a man fallen drunk and asleep on the side of the road; in other words, a fresh kill. Shouts of conquest rang through the dark forest at strange intervals and shook the blackbirds from the trees, and Horace noticed, after an hour or two, that he hadn't come upon any magical creatures. No trolls, no giants, not even a partially enchanted snail crossed his path. The only sign that magic still inhabited the forest, and hadn't fled altogether, was the small patch of violet flowers that sprung up behind Horace as he walked, but of these Horace passed unaware, for he had no occasion to look back.

CHAPTER TWELVE

At noon, Horace entered a clearing where two knights, arrayed in horsehair headdresses and gleaming, bejeweled breastplates, faced one another with staves like peasant fighters. Their squires stood watching a ways back in the road, both with their knight's sword at the ready, and as Horace was not wearing his own armor, and as he was leading Lazarus because he still had not learned to ride, the two lads mistook him for a squire, and greeted him as such. "Where's your knight?" they wanted to know. "Was he just defeated?" Horace meant to tell them all of it, but when he opened his mouth to begin he discovered he was too tired for it, and so instead he only nodded and turned his attention towards the fight. And that's when he recognized the Red Knight by his bulbous, florid nose.

"Blackheart! How dare you put yourself forward to defend the princess! She shall have no champion the likes of you!" the Red Knight howled. He swung his stave over his head in a grand display of knightly acrobatics, stamped his foot, and howled again.

"Foul beast!" the other man shouted. "Impudent cur! False pretender to the quest! How dare you show your face in this forest!" The knight shoved the blunt end of his stave directly into the Red Knight's gut. It occurred to Horace then that one of these lads was the Red Knight's squire, exactly as he had once been. The squires both flinched, but neither made any move towards the battle, either to aid or to dispel, so it was several more blows, flinches, and shouts before Horace could determine which squire stood for the Red Knight in his old place. "Dishonorable worm!" the knight in black shouted. He landed a final blow at the Red Knight's temple, and the man's knees buckled. He swayed for a moment between consciousness and sleep, and then with a crack like the snap of a tree trunk, he fell face down in the dirt.

"Well that's that." One of the squires followed the Black Knight off down the trail, but the other knelt beside the Red Knight with a broken piece of mirror that he held to the man's nose. He balanced the shard of glass perfectly in the knight's bushy beard. "One moment." He held his hand out to keep Horace back. "I've seen so many dead knights, I had to find a trick to make sure they were really dead, if you know what I mean."

"Sure," Horace offered a hand to help the squire to his feet. "The kingdom must be running short on them by now."

"Exactly." The squire looked at Horace with a side eye and said, "Say, you aren't one of the Duke of Loraine's, are you?" He glanced at Lazarus, and then at the saddle bag packed to bulging with gold plate armor. Something about Horace didn't add up.

"No, nothing like that." Horace stooped to wrap his arms around the Red Knight's barrel chest. "Heft up his feet and help me move him to the meadow. We'll bury him over by that tree." The squire did as Horace asked, for Horace's tone was authoritative enough and the squire liked to do as he was told. He ran to fetch axes from stray battle sites he remembered passing that morning, and the two of them made quick work of digging the Red Knight's grave, chopping away at the dirt. Once they'd given the Red Knight a proper burial, Horace told the squire what he considered to be the best version of the truth: "I am a knight of the Kingdom of Prester John."

"Oh?" The squire tossed the Red Knight's broken stave on the fire. "Where's that?"

"In the east, where the sun rises. Some say at the end of the world, but I prefer to think it's at the beginning." The squire nodded in polite silence, and Horace thought the better of such poetic descriptions and changed his tone and his story, to some extent. "Prester John has knowledge of the enchantment that bewitches the princess, and he has sent me with the antidote."

The squire cocked his head to the side as if thinking of an objection. "If you're a knight of this John fellow, then where's your squire? Where's your armor and weapons? Why don't you look like a knight?"

Lazarus snorted, and Horace chuckled. "My armor is in that saddle bag; you can see there are more than a few casks of cheese in there, and you know as well as I do a man with no squire can't dress himself."

"Where's your squire then?"

"He was eaten by a dragon when we crossed the Deepest Lake in the World."

They sat together companionably for a while, poking at

the embers of the dying fire, and then Horace said, "You know, I was a squire once, in the Red Knight's household. It was from a knight named Lazarus that I first received my arms, and it is of this country that I was born. Had I not left his service when he refused the quest, I would still be a squire today. I would be you."

"And I would still be on the dung heap," said the squire. "Say, my name's Yorick."

"Horace." They shook hands.

"Horace, I don't suppose you'd want to take on a squire, you know, someone to help you put on your armor and whatnot. Chivalry is a two-man business, they say."

And so it happened that when Horace entered the capital of the kingdom he was clad in gleaming gold armor, mounted, tenuously, on the finest white steed, and served by a squire beaming with pride for the exploits of his knight, but a lot of good it did him for there was no one at the castle gate. News had come that morning that the Duke of Loraine, tired of waiting for Angelica's acquiescence, would soon give the order for his mercenary army to stream over the border and destroy everything in their wake. Horace, with Yorick tramping through the mud of the neglected streets, entered a city in chaos. Men and women shoved one another as they scurried to hide their belongings from the approaching army. A woman with a chicken in a cage ran into Lazarus's hindquarters and spooked the horse so badly he reared back and screamed. For the moment, everyone in earshot fell silent and waited, watching the wild horse to see what it would do. Horace saw an opportunity, and he took it.

"People of Angleterre!" he shouted, "I am sent by his holiness, guardian of the gates of the East, the legendary and noble Prester John!" and here a worried hush ran through the crowd, for who, besides Yorick, has not heard of the legendary Prester John? "I come to break the terrible enchantment that troubles this land!"

Yorick hissed, "What do you think you're doing?" but Horace shot him a look that made him straighten up quick. It wasn't, after all, a lie, at least it wasn't in the sense that Horace had just come from Prester John's kingdom and had a relative degree of faith in his instructions, simple though they may be. And it must have worked, too, for soon a crowd had gathered around them, whatever cause they had for hurry seemingly forgotten. Horace, who hadn't thought much beyond his initial shout, floundered and stuttered and would have blown the whole thing, had Yorick not stepped in.

"That's right!" Yorick shouted. "I have followed this noble knight for many hours and what he says is the truth! A braver man there never was, and I say to you now that if he is presented to the king this instant, the princess will be restored in a matter of days. Make haste, good people!"

The crowd murmured, collectively chewing over their options, and Yorick turned to Horace to say, "Now what?" when they both were saved by a member of the king's guard who happened to be passing by an arched window in the castle keep and leaned his head out to see what all the commotion was about. He sent word to the men at the gate to quiet the fellow who was causing unrest by screaming about the possibility of relief, and so it happened that Horace and Yorick, within a matter of minutes, were escorted through the city gates and into the castle courtyard proper, Horace still mounted on Lazarus as due the honor of a true knight, and Yorick leading the horse by the reins.

Angelica looked out the window of her father's council room with smug disdain in her eyes. "What's all that racket?" she said, to no one in particular. As was often the case with Angelica, teams of people swarmed around her but not one of them had anything to say that was helpful. Her ladies, the twelve chattering fools the council forced on her after that May Day morning when, from her own perspective, she'd finally came to her senses, all hurried to the window to bow and scrape and curtsy and peer at the two men in the courtyard that seemed to hold Angelica's interest, but none of them knew anything about it. "Why can't I have a conversation, just once," she moaned, to no one in particular, "with someone who knows something?" And with that she glanced at her fat, lazy father, the only person in the kingdom who could claim to outrank her. I tell you in the strictest confidence that she was hoping for a reprimand from her father for her rudeness to her ladies, but none was forthcoming, for the king, propped up on his throne by a pillow, had fallen asleep. "Agh! I'm surrounded by incompetence!" she shrieked, and picked up the nearest handy volume to hurl out the window at the crowd below. Her ladies in waiting, like the people in the street thronging around Horace and Yorick, scattered.

Yorick stooped to pick the book up since no one else was willing, but as he was only a squire he immediately turned it over to Horace, who thumbed through the volume quickly, then tucked it into the breastplate of his armor. It was a collection of poems written some time before in honor of a beautiful woman, and the less said about that, the better. What matters in the here and now of the dirty courtyard of King Mark's castle, with war looming on the horizon and the princess raging upstairs, is that Horace kept them close to his heart. Indeed, he had always, but that is a matter only an alchemist can understand.

It was noon and so the court gates opened to admit knights returning from the King's Great Quest, as the people had become accustomed to calling it. Two men in the purple livery of the nobles of Angleterre, trumpets at their side, threw open the formal court doors that separated the main courtyard of the palace from the royal family's receiving room. The trumpets reared back like horses, their songs blasted like honking geese, and a diminutive man in fancy particolored hose stepped out into the courtyard sunlight. He unfurled a thick scroll with much ceremony and read from it in a swinging, swaggering way, all the other people gathered in the courtyard mumbling along with the words. They heard it read every day, at exactly the same time, in exactly the same way, like clockwork. If they ever really wanted to listen to it, they only had to wait for the time to come around again.

"… and in solitude, and peace, and comfort, and prosperity, as long as the Lord of Heaven grant us all these boons," he concluded, followed immediately by a great flourish of trumpets and the exclamation, "People of Angleterre, make way for the knights of the realm!" After this the man paused, but only briefly. So certain was he that no knight would come forward, as none had for weeks and weeks and months, that the alchemist turned almost immediately on his heel and was halfway back through the arched doorway when he heard someone call out, "Wait!"

It was Yorick. He stood panting and gesturing back at

Horace, who watched, a little slow to understand what was happening, from his horse. "A knight!" he gasped, panicked. "Here is a knight!" Horace blushed red as a radish when all eyes turned towards him, including a certain pair of blue eyes watching, with marginal interest, from the open windows billowing soft violet draperies above.

"Is there a knight?" the alchemist said, peering over the half-rolled scroll and up his nose at Horace, a posture, as you can imagine, that was no more comfortable than it was common to the man, who was far more used to looking down at people.

Horace smiled sheepishly, the village wives would later say humbly, and raised his hand, a bit timidly, and if it was shaking, well, no extant source made a record of that. "There is," was all he said.

"Then," said the alchemist, "by all means, come with me." The officious man sneered at Yorick. "You will tether your horse here, if you don't mind." Horace nodded and trembled all the more. Now came the moment Horace most dreaded. He cast his eyes about for any way around it, but no solution presented itself, and not for lack of faith on Horace's part that some better option would appear at the very last moment. It did not. Sighing and resigned, Horace slid from the side of the horse to his feet and faced the crowd, the alchemist, and the pair of pretty eyes watching from behind the violet curtains high above, with every bit of height that he could muster. All sixty inches.

CHAPTER THIRTEEN

People were generally shorter in ages past. The exact cause for our dramatic rise over the centuries has yet to be determined; some say government physical fitness programs, some say toxic waste. Only time will tell. What matters here, in the center of Angleterre at the epicenter of the country's most dire political crisis, is that Horace was a full head shorter than any other man looking at him, and a full head shorter, more to the point, than any woman.

Angelica turned away from the window, bored by everything. "You," she snapped at one of her father's council members. "I want to be entertained. Organize a tournament."

"Your majesty." The courtier removed his fox fur hat and the afternoon sunlight reflected off the curve of his bald head. "Pardon me, your majesty, but what kind of tournament would most amuse you? We have a fascinating chess rivalry brewing in the salon, and the expense of a tournament of real combat, the men alone..."

"What does it matter?" Angelica snapped, and the man bowed and slunk back into the crowd of mingling court hangers-on and social climbers. There was no one in the room who really wanted to be there, Angelica thought as she looked down over the courtyard again. There was no one in the courtyard to watch but an old man pushing a wheelbarrow, the wheel toothed by missing spokes, forcing his heap of dung through the ruts left in the mud by people and beasts.

Horace, with Yorick just behind, followed the alchemist through the maze of interconnected receiving rooms, ball salons and stinking scullery alcoves. The alchemist walked with the prim half measured step of a bride on her wedding day, so they had plenty of time to observe in minutiae everything as they walked behind him. Of particular interest was the hall of arms, a sacred place to those who dream of knighthood with its row upon row of noble shields patent. Even the words used to classify patents in the hall of arms were ancient and serious: argent on a fess sable three bezants between three fleur-de-lys gules. Horace's hand touched, unbidden, unconscious, the outline of the earthworm on his chest. They were just weapons, no more noble or mysterious than his own. Maybe less so. He sighed, and Yorick grabbed a hunk of chainmail hanging from his shirtwaist and yanked him back, hissing in his ear: "What's wrong? Not having second thoughts, are you?"

Horace only shook him off. The memory of Angelica's musical laughter flitted around in his head like a flutterby, but that didn't mean she'd fall in love with him just because it was convenient for him and just because he was there. The earthworm, whatever it was, hadn't given him any clues. "This is hopeless." At the top of the twentieth flight of stairs, he sat down and refused to stand back up again. Yorick had to run after the alchemist to ask him please to wait.

The alchemist ignored Yorick, as if speaking to him were something of a fool's errand. He turned instead, retraced his steps down several feet to Horace's level, and looked down on the hunched shoulders of the melancholy knight.

Horace shrugged. "What difference does it make?" Behind him, Yorick looked around, making a mental checklist of all the escape routes in the stairway. But Horace wasn't disturbed by the alchemist's nosy stare and bossy attitude at all. The only thing that scared Horace was the passage of time.

Then the alchemist did something surprising and altogether out of character: he clapped his hands together with a rapturous look and cried out, "Marvelous! I had myself so convinced it couldn't be that I scarcely dared to hope…"

"Couldn't be what?" Yorick said.

The alchemist shot a look at Yorick that could be translated, roughly, as "Quiet, you!" Then he turned his gaze back on Horace, or Horace's earthworm-engraved breastplate, and said in a voice dripping with honey: "Where did you acquire your arms?"

Horace looked the alchemist directly in the eye and said, "What difference does that make?"

"All the difference in the world, dear boy! The earthworm is, that is to say it was, although scholars certainly dispute this and there's room for debate on both sides, but… well, that is I mean," and then he hopped up and down in a most unalchemistic manner and gasped, "It would be so much easier if I showed you. Come!" and then he turned and shooed Yorick further up the stairs. "Come on, time is wasting!"

131

He took them to a room in the tallest tower of the castle, a small, squat door huddled under the shambles of an eve, holes in the stone work at odd moments that spoke to centuries of war rot and weather damage in its past. The alchemist drew a chain from beneath his fluffed, lacy collar, dangling a collection of keys as small and as thin as teeth. Into the padlock that affixed two rusted chains he inserted one, pressed his tongue through his lips as he turned the key in the tiny lock, and opened the door. A rush of cold air blasted by them, and they could see through the doorway that the far wall of the room was a large window bright with sunlight, large enough for a man to step through, and indeed there was nothing to prevent a person, save his or her own good sense, from stepping out over the edge of the ledge and tumbling more than a thousand feet to his or her death.

"Funny," Yorick said, peering through the massive window. "It all looks so different from up here."

The alchemist smiled, and his eyes sparkled with the soon-to-be revealed. Then Horace shoved Yorick aside, mouth gaping, and ran into the room ahead of them both. At the far window there was a contraption just like the one in the high tower of Prester John's kingdom, and when I say just like I am not precise because the fact of the matter is that it wasn't like Prester John's pulley system, it was Prester John's pulley system. Horace gazed down in wonder at the empty gleaming cobblestone streets, the squat brick wall on the horizon. Somehow, this was the tower in Prester John's kingdom.

"I'm sure you know where you are," the alchemist said, and closed the door on Angleterre. Yorick clung to the wall for safety against the whipping wind, but Horace stood in the window, on the ledge, one hand examining the harness dangling from the pulley. "I don't understand," he said.

"Of course you don't, it hasn't been explained to you."

Horace stooped down, scanning the city streets for any sign of the old monk making his way through the pristine cobblestone courtyards in his ratty blue robes, but if Prester John were indeed in the city below, Horace didn't see him. Far in the distance the garden wall waited.

The alchemist didn't bother to wait for Horace to ask for further elaboration. "This is what men in the future will call a portal. I know that because I've been to the future to collect nomenclature. Terrible place. Full of advertisements."

"What's an advertisement?" Yorick asked from the safety of the wall, his voice drowned out by the thunder of the wind.

"It's like a coat of arms for a company." Yorick thought that by a company, the alchemist meant a group of men working towards a common goal, which was correct in a sense, and so everyone was satisfied by the explanation, and the alchemist went on. "A portal works like a doorway, you merely open it and step through. When we walked into this room, we walked into Prester John's kingdom. When we walk out again, we'll be back in the Kingdom of Mark."

"I don't understand why you're showing me this." Horace leaned his head against the frame of the window. More than any-

133

thing, he wanted to glide down the line to the garden and slip back into the flowers, where things made sense.

The alchemist put his hand on Horace's shoulder. "You've been here before, haven't you?"

"Yes, but how did you know?"

"That's the emblem of Prester John, isn't it?" The alchemist's eyes went to Horace's breastplate, the earthworm emblazoned there.

Horace ran his thumb over the raised outline of the earthworm's face, looked down at the inlaid carving. "Of course," he said. "Of course it is."

The alchemist went to get a book down from one of the shelves near the doorway, where the volumes were held in place against the wind only by sheer force of number, so crammed into the wooden shelves they were. The book was a thick volume of illuminated pages, and when he brought it back to Horace, it was open on a page with several permutations of the earthworm crest, as well as annotations of who had worn the emblem, when, and for what duration. "The last time this realm saw a Knight of the Garden," he said, "was more than a thousand years ago. So you can imagine my delight…"

Horace took the book from the alchemist and read the ornate handwritten description at the lower right-hand side of the page. The hand was so archaic, it took a while for Horace to recognize some of the letters, let alone the words, but as he sounded each one out, their meaning took shape. What they said was this:

"The Knights of the Garden are alone in all the chivalrous orders, in that they receive their arms from no human hand and are instead knighted by fate. It is useless to seek admission; when one is selected, his arms come to him as if by chance or happenstance. The scholar Phoebus conjectures..." and here Horace read no further, for the conjectures of scholars were nothing to him.

"I have every confidence," the alchemist said, in a hushed, reverent whisper quite drowned out by the whipping wind, "that you can restore this kingdom to peace and prosperity. And moreover, so does he." With this, the alchemist made a grandiose gesture toward the garden wall, and at that exact moment, as if by miracle or intelligent design, a sunbeam broke through the clouds and shone down on Horace's face.

"I don't have any instructions," Horace protested. "It said something about psychosis and some other bit I don't quite remember..."

"Psychosis?" The alchemist turned again to the shelf of books. "I'm not familiar with that term, is it Gaelic?"
Yorick, who had watched all of this with ill-concealed disbelief, more convinced than ever his betters had played an elaborate joke on him, said "Maybe it's from the future."

"Possibly," the alchemist said, and Yorick looked back and forth between them as if they'd both gone mad while the alchemist scanned the titles on the shelf, occasionally pulling one loose to thumb through it, then shoving it back into place with an annoyed mumble. "If so it may take a day or two to locate any material on the subject."

"A day or two. Of course," said Yorick.

Horace stood, put his hand on the wire, tested its weight. More than anything, he wanted to strap himself into the harness and glide down to the ground, where he was sure Prester John would meet him and open the gate to paradise. But the alchemist was right; there was the quest, and apparently it had chosen him as its champion. The time for gardens would come again, as it always did. "Never mind that," Horace said. "Take me to the princess."

Yorick grinned. "Now that's more like it. Action, not useless words and scholarship." The alchemist looked at Yorick like he smelled bad, but Yorick only bowed and opened the door for them both. Soon the tower door closed behind them, and locked, and they were in Angleterre again, just as they had been before, although everything from the castle walls to the decorative carpets carried a faint haze of blue for the next few minutes, suggesting none of it was real.

The princess Angelica, at that exact moment, was overseeing arrangements for her tournament, and very much engrossed in the selection of the prizes. "I want organza leaf for the medals," she said, and leaned over the table to finger the flimsy roll of Irish lace spread across it. "Last time it was cheap cotton gauze and you all tried to tell me it was not."

Johnson Proudhouse, in happier times the King's aide-de-camp, bowed his head a little lower and removed the offensive cloth, turning to shove it into the arms of a waiting woman who frantically ran out the back door with it. It was his studied opinion that nothing was wrong with the princess that a marriage and a few children couldn't solve, and he'd said so, time and time again as the council gathered around the war room table plotting strategies to bring the long, oppressive winter of no central leadership to its end; but they squabbled, as they always did without Angelica's wise guidance, and nothing was ever accomplished.

"But I can hardly think of how the winner should be recognized." Angelica pushed aside the hammered gold trophy someone neglected to take away. "We made the last tourney winner a baron, and Papa was quite put out; he said he'd run out of land if I created any more barons, and they'd be wanting to disturb his sleep. But we can't afford to give out any more stallions…"

It was idle chatter, just something to pass the afternoon away, the thought of a tournament, and once the tournament had come and gone, there would have to be another to plan, or a ball, or some other diversion, unless of course there was finally a war. Messages came from the Loraine front every day about the movement of the Duke's men along the border, and none of them so frightening as the report that Loraine himself, arraigned in gleaming armor, had taken to riding up and down the lists, rallying the men. Soon he would cross the border, and then all would be lost.

"Perhaps your hand, princess," Johnson Proudhouse said, and bowed almost low enough to scrape the floor before he looked back to see what her reaction had been.

"I thought you'd promised my hand off already, to whoever completes that quest of yours." She waved her hand about dismissively and turned back to the book of arms someone had thrust under her nose, the suggestion being that she revive the dead line of some old family.

"Yes, but, well, don't you think the quest is just a tad bit... impossible?"

There was a murmur of discontent throughout the room, as if Proudhouse had committed a grave and offensive sacrilege.

"You mean to suggest, sir, that our knights are not capable of completing the quest?"

"The nerve!"

"The very idea! A man of state!"

And so on and so forth the courtiers grumbled, until Proudhouse managed to get them to quiet down just long enough to listen to his defense. "Look out the eastern windows! Listen to the cries that rise daily from the Forbidden Forest! They're just fighting one another out there and they have been doing nothing else but for months!"

"Heretic!"

"Burn him!"

Proudhouse looked around the room for someone to speak up for him, for one sane person to admit that they ought to think about what he was saying, because after all it was the truth, but none were willing to stick their neck out so far that the princess might see her way clear to chop through it, and so they held their peace. A contingency of guards was called, and they marched in and dragged the poor Proudhouse away. As he was being taken away, the alchemist was bringing Horace in, and the two groups passed each other in the hallway. For a brief moment their eyes met, Horace and Proudhouse's, although what was communicated in that moment is hard to describe. Horace passed the unfortunate man with the distinct impression that something very precious and central to the national character would be lost before too long, if no one put a stop to it.

The alchemist had the guards push open the double doors of the room with as much ceremony and theater as they could muster, and two trumpeters appeared by magic; this combined with the alchemist's foppish and studied manner of calling attention to himself created quite a show for the people milling around in the princess's court; and, it should be noted, since Angelica had fallen under the enchantment of narcissism, she had been particularly susceptible to the alchemist's officious brand of pomp and circumstance. She took her seat on her father's throne immediately and watched with the same hushed reverence as the lesser mortals of the room when the alchemist began his speech.

I will not bore you with the alchemist's speech. Suffice to say it was long, ornate, and made the intended impression; when Horace stepped forward and took his knee before the princess, it no longer mattered to any in the room that he was shorter than most older children and had fewer connections; all they saw was a legendary hero returned from an epic quest; in other words, the alchemist made them suspend disbelief for as long as it took to believe Horace was what he said he was, a true hero.

Angelica swallowed nervously. She could not remember if she had ever been in the presence of a man who had enacted such noble deeds. "You may rise knight and greet us." She hoped her tone was at its most haughty and disdainful. It wouldn't do to let him know how anxious he made her feel. She looked down in her lap and realized she had shredded the bit of tissue paper some councilor gave her for a fabric sample.

Horace stood, but didn't say anything at all. He merely nodded his head, partially in assent, partially in greeting, as if he would conserve his words and deploy them carefully, and Angelica longed to hear his voice. It made her angry that he withheld it from her. "Speak!" she snapped, finally, as though his presence were the most annoying thing in the world when the truth couldn't be farther from it, and when he didn't say anything, but only looked at her with eyes like sleeping flowers, she stood up from her throne and shouted, "What? What is it? Is that what you came all this way for? Just to look at me?"

The entire collection of court hangers-on cowered under her hurled words, but Horace watched her, waiting for her to stop screaming. And once she did (he didn't know what drove him, for God knows it wasn't the confidence of experience) what Horace said was, "and to win the tournament you're planning."

"The tournament?" For the moment she'd forgotten about the tournament. She took her throne, then, to compose herself. "Very well. Go and rest yourself in one of the court compartments. I will have the bailiff assign you rooms. Have you got a horse?" He nodded the affirmative and she continued, "I'll see that he is fed and combed and given a stall in the stables. And your squire?"

Horace gestured to the door, five hundred yards or so behind him, and Angelica said, "He will have a bed and a bowl in the hall with the others. Is there anything else?" Horace thanked her for her generosity. "Go then," she said, and he turned and strode from the room. Once he'd gone, she said in an offhanded way to one of the councilors, "We will offer our hand to the winner. It pleases me."

Everyone whispered that the short, silent man must be some sort of sorcerer. How else could he bewitch the princess so? The alchemist listened to their gossip with glee. Horace was a true knight, and here was the proof of it. It was a subject that fascinated him endlessly, and like a horticulturalist gathering specimens, he happily considered the implications of his observations on the subject and discovered a handful of new questions to ruminate over and pursue. In short, he could not be happier than he was in the present.

The morning of the tournament dawned stony gray with a dark wind from the west, and the blackbirds cried in the cattle shed. The old wives said it was Black Friday, but whether they meant to suggest that the day would see great sacrifice, or only that it actually was Black Friday, our history does not record. What it does record is this: when the sun finally broke through the clouds, Horace stood with creaking knees from his position at the foot of the chapel altar and kissed his sword.

Victory was imminent.

The tournament in the Markist period was not unlike the Hollywood movie of which modern readers are familiar. Twelve knights marched their mounts before the king and princess for their review, two by two with a military cadence, before splitting off into lists. Jousts were first, as they were the deadliest and commonly eliminated at least half the field. Once the yard was cleared of that debris, swords followed, then daggers, shaving razors, and sometimes lady's hairpins, culminating at last in hand-to-hand combat if any challengers at all remained.

There were, as it happened, none.

Horace came out ahead in the jousts, which was a shock. Before Yorick handed him his spear, he said to him, "Boss, just don't tuck in and protect your neck. That's how they always get thrown off, they protect the neck." Horace, who had never jousted before, and still did not know how to ride, but had squired long enough to agree with Yorick, nodded and took the lance. It was three passes of holding on for dear life before he threw the first one, and by then he'd found the rhythm. Lazarus had charged in many a tournament, and he took care of the rest.

Two more times they squared off, and twice more their opponent landed in the dirt. None died, and later legend would attribute that to the especially moral tone of the day, for Horace had a kind of glow about him that inspired the halos that illuminated saints in later manuscripts. When they brought him to the dais to be toasted, all the women in the crowd whispered that he looked like Prester John himself.

And maybe he did, a little. Angelica certainly thought so, when she laid the wreath of honor on his neck during the noontime awards ceremony. Something in her stirred her to touch his cheek, but she held back, not quite sure why. In the stands she heard ladies whispering and giggling; on her way back to her throne, she shot them a look that would peel paint off a plastic wall. "I am nothing of the kind," she said, icily, to the first person to remark on her flush and its origins. "It's just terribly hot today. Fetch me a cold cloth before I faint." She flung herself down on the throne next to her father and made a big show of not even watching when Horace came to the field with his dagger to face his opponent for the next round. Just to show all of them. Horace especially.

Then it happened. Horace and his opponent, Lars Marymaker of the far north, squared off against one another in the freshly-cleared field, each with a shaving razor firmly clutched in his strong right hand. Lars was a large man, no larger than your average-sized large man, but when he stood next to Horace, he looked huge. At first, this seemed to give Horace the advantage. Lars thrust forward too quickly in the opening movements of the fight, got caught in his own momentum, and suffered several serious slashes to the backs of his thighs as Horace ducked and ran behind him.

Angelica's hand reached out for her father's when the first blow struck. Fat, Stupid King Mark was dozing, sitting bolt upright in his chair as if one of his courtiers had tied his hair to the banner behind him, his mouth hanging open, and when Angelica squeezed his hand he jerked awake. "What? Who's calling me?" he said. Just then Horace lunged forward a second too early, tripped over the giant's massive foot, and was rewarded with a fist to the jaw. Angelica gasped and leaned towards the bloody battlefield, and Mark smiled. He took his daughter's hand, the way he used to do when she was a child. "Don't worry dear," Stupid King Mark said, "I'm sure that young man will come out alright in the end."

Angelica smiled at her father, for he did have kind eyes, and then turned back towards the field where Horace had rallied far enough to dig the blade of his razor into the giant's palm. Marymaker howled with pain and lashed out at Horace with his other hand, slashing right and left while Horace jumped and dodged, trying to grab his razor back. Angelica jumped to her feet. "Do something!" she cried out, to no one and to everyone, although in hindsight it appears that she addressed her pleas to King Mark. Just then, the blade connected with Horace's throat, slashed a vein in his neck, and sprayed blood all over the field.

Time stood still. And then time ran, and it was Angelica running, the hem of her skirt caught and torn on a stray sword handle before she reached her champion lying in a pool of his own, warm blood. She heard shouting, and the giant, lost in the frenzy of the kill, had to be dragged off of her, by whom she never knew. The sight of Horace's eyes as the life drained from them chilled her. She knelt beside him; it was plain he wanted to say something, but no sound escaped his lips, so she pressed her lips to his forehead and whispered, "I love you." He smiled at her, and then he was gone.

CHAPTER FOURTEEN

Horace's death was a terrible loss for the kingdom, even Stupid King Mark knew that. At the alchemist's suggestion, and with Angelica's consent, the council declared a public day of mourning for the dung peddler's son, complete with hired wailing women, a fourteen piece marching band to parade his body through the city streets—with tuba— and a ticker tape brigade sprinkling office garbage from the parapets of the castle like rose petals. Angelica watched from her room in the tower as the procession passed under her window. Yorick led the parade in his most solid, dignified manner, glancing over his shoulder occasionally to make sure Horace's golden coffin hadn't tumbled or shuddered behind him as the attendants, squires of other knights lost to the quest, picked their way through the numerous potholes and muddy rivulets in the streets. For Horace was truly dead, and never coming back, as much as you or I or Angelica might wish it. It was the finality of his death more than anything else that shook Angelica back to her senses. She had loved, a little, and now there was nothing to keep her mind off it but work.

She turned away from the window in the high tower and towards her mirror, and her reflection still surprised. Her hair, the riotous blonde locks, the source of so much vanity in her self-centered days, had turned bright white overnight, and were now shot through with silvery gray threads that made her look, if not less beautiful, then much more wise than before. Her skin, still young and dewy, had taken on creases at the eyes that made her worries easier to trace and her smiles hardier and easier to enjoy. And if she smiled more frequently these days, she had to be forgiven. Anyone who has loved and lost knows that life is precious, and Angelica was generally more wise about the twists and turns in life than most. And so it was that on the fourth day of the second month of the fortieth year of the reign of Stupid King Mark, Angelica bound her white hair in a tidy, utilitarian bun at the base of her neck, asked her staff for a simple black dress, and went downstairs to take up the serious business of running the state.

"I see God's hand in this," Stupid King Mark told his council when Angelica entered the war room laden with charts and maps and books and opinions. Even Stupid King Mark got it right once in a while. Whether or not God has hands, strictly speaking, is another matter.

Angelica spread her research materials across the large oak table, one long scrolling map unrolling so far it slumped over the end of the table and dangled halfway off the ground, while Angelica waited for the excited murmuring gossip to die down. "I've been digging around in the war room, and this is my conclusion. We have to build a wall."

"Preposterous!" A man so fat his rotund girth hugged both top and bottom of the table when he bruited up against it leaned close to Angelica. "A project like that would bankrupt the treasury!"

"Good money after bad," a second, prim and razor-thin courtier agreed.

"And with no proof that such an operation could even be profitable…" said a third, somewhat smaller courtier, sandwiched between the very fat man and the very thin one.

"Can it be a brick wall?" Stupid King Mark said in his sleep.

"Of course it can, Daddy. It can be whatever you like as long as it's sturdy under cannon fire." She unrolled a greenprint (blueprints were green in those days because blue or black ink hadn't been invented yet, which made signing official government documents very difficult) and showed them how a wall might be erected just shy of the border of Loraine and used as a battlement from which to fight and face the enemy, like the Great Wall of China, which was coincidentally being pitched to the Chinese Emperor in red ink at that very same moment. "And so you can see," Angelica stared down the fat councilor with a look of dangerous ire she'd perfected in her selfish days, "this is the only plan that can stop the Duke of Loraine's saber-rattling for good. Unless any of you have any better ideas." The fat councilor knew better than to suggest that she marry the Duke of Loraine, which honestly was the most elegant solution from the perspective of the tax payer, but absolutely out of the question, and so better left unsaid.

Construction of the Great Wall of Angleterre would begin that very afternoon, after the builder's guild and the quarry guild and the stonemason's guild and the architect's guild were consulted, and each had argued for and eventually given up on their own, more pressing pet projects, and after Angelica had secured the support of the knights, who would of course have to fight from the top of the thing and would want to know how they were expected

147

to get their horses all the way up there. It also meant a visit to the alchemist, who twitched oddly and glanced distractedly through his tower window every time Angelica said the word "wall".

"What the devil are you looking at?" Two hours of his distracted evasion drove Angelica to a fit of pique.

"Nothing, nothing... only..." the alchemist traced his finger around the base of his decorative (which means empty) wine glass. "Only... did you get this idea from Horace?"

"Horace?" Angelica was sure she blushed. "What the devil do you mean by that?" Angelica was inordinately fascinated with the devil after she'd emerged from her brief sojourn into selfishness. It was to become the subject of much debate in the pseudo-psychological societies that arose in the coming decades.

"I mean," the alchemist cleared his throat and fumbled with the books on his desk, stalling. Just then, Yorick burst through the door, unannounced, carrying a taxidermied snow owl.

"The best I could do on such short notice," he shrugged, and put it on the bookcase near the window that the alchemist threw so many nervous glances towards in Angelica's presence. "I'll go out for another, if you want. I don't mind."

The alchemist waved his suggestion away. "No, no lad, that'll do well enough. Leave us now." Yorick nodded, and would have left, but Angelica stopped him.

"Wait! Aren't you the squire of Horace?"

Yorick glanced at the alchemist, who nodded as if to say 'Go on and tell her, if you want,' and so he made a humble little bow for the princess and introduced himself. "At your service," he said, and kissed her outstretched hand.

"I've been looking all over for you!" Angelica stood up so quickly she knocked her greenprints and charts all over the floor. "I have to know what happened on the quest! Horace never had a chance to tell me, the poor man."

Yorick flushed red. "I was only his squire the last two days of it," he stammered. "I wasn't with him the entire way. I've never actually been out of Angleterre."

"Is that so…" Angelica turned away from the two exasperating men, looking out the tower window that seemed to make the alchemist so nervous. She didn't know why it should be so; it was just the same as the window in her own tower room, just the same luxurious position above the fray. Angelica held her hand above her eyes to ward off the glaring noon day sun, which from this great height seemed to be no more than a football field away, however far that was. "What is that?" she said after a minute more of staring at the horizon, blinking in the sunlight. "Did someone manage to get the wall built without me?"

"You've been through a trauma, we all have." Yorick put his arm on her elbow, the way one does when it's necessary to lead an elderly relative away from the computer or some other danger. "Let me make you a nice cup of tea." Angelica shook him off. She was no longer in the mood to be babied.

"There's a wall in the distance. I can see it plain as day. Except there is no wall in the distance, so what the devil am I looking at?"

"It's not of the devil," the alchemist insisted. After a few more minutes glaring and prodding and insisting, he sighed and gave in. "It's not even of Angleterre. That window doesn't look out over your kingdom, your Majesty. It looks over the kingdom of Prester John."

Angelica gaped at the little man, and never had he felt so little in his life. "Are you telling me," she said, slowly, "that one can physically reach the Kingdom of Prester John by climbing through this window?"

"More gliding, really." Yorick tugged on the imperceptibly thin wire that stretched from the far wall through the window and into infinity.

"Prudence, now." The alchemist tried to slam the curtains shut on his portal. "It isn't that simple, there are guidelines and traditions that govern..."

Angelica thrust the little man back and threw open the curtains again. A white light more pure and concentrated than sunlight flooded the room. "You mean that anyone, anyone can just zip on down to the Kingdom of Prester John anytime he wants? What the, I mean why'd we even have a quest, entertainment?"

"Certainly not." The alchemist was grunting now, hopping about on his slim, stocking feet and acting more agitated than anyone had seen him in years. "For one, not just anyone can go..."

but then he seemed to have stepped in the way of revealing more secrets, so he stopped talking and went about the room making a show of locking up the other windows. "Yorick, be a good lad and go and get my compendium."

Angelica shook with anger. "All those men fighting and dying in the Forbidden Forest, and all you had to do…"

Yorick returned with a book so large it had to be balanced and carried atop his head, and the alchemist shrugged out of Angelica's grip and smoothed down his collar in an effort to regain his composure. "I believe," he said, in a soft respectful tone, thumbing through the crackling pages of the enormous, ancient book, "that you share some of that burden as well."

A month before, Angelica would have had the man set out in the stocks for his insolence, and a year before that she would have swallowed her pride and let reflection turn her mistake into valuable experience, but this was in the here and now, and neither there nor then, so present day Angelica said, "You know, I came to see you because I thought I needed your support to build a wall. But now I just need to go through that window."

"Why?" The alchemist had reached the page where the coat of arms of the Kingdom of Prester John was described, the same page he'd shown Horace only a few days before. Angelica watched as he ran his fingers across the fresh ink that inscribed Horace's name there as one of the knights of that fabled kingdom, testing to see if it had dried. "There's no guarantee you'll find anything on the other side of the line. I've seen many a knight climb through that window, never to return."

151

"What happens to them?"

The alchemist shrugged. "I can't say. The only one who's ever come back from Prester John's Kingdom in my lifetime was Horace. And he came back on foot."

"Minus his squire."

"Yes, of course Yorick. Minus his squire." The alchemist turned the book towards Angelica, and when she touched the ancient page, imperceptible flowers, microscopic and almost transparent in their violet color, bloomed and died in the wake of her fingerprints.

"I'll need a squire if I'm going to survive the return journey. You can be my squire, Yorick." Angelica had a plain way of stating matters of grave political implication, and for the first several minutes the two men refused to believe they had heard her correctly. The wind whistled at the window overlooking the Kingdom of Prester John.

In the far distance sighed a faint murmur of a million tiny voices, singing.

"But why, princess? Why go to Prester John's Kingdom? Why now when the country is falling apart and the people need you to lead them?"

The alchemist folded his arms across his chest. "It won't bring him back, you know."

"I know," Angelica said. She walked over to the window and looked out through the blinding white light cast by the collusion of space and time. "But there's something there waiting for me, something only I can bring back. I think I've been given a quest."

"You know I can't sanction it." The alchemist closed the mighty book. Nowhere in its pages did it even suggest that a woman might attain, nevertheless be called to, the ranks of the chivalrous. "But you have my support for the wall. I'll create a noble order and the men will be killing one another for the honor of its insignia before sunset tomorrow."

"No, no killing. Find another way to motivate the men, but no more killing."

The alchemist shot a glance at Yorick, who would understand better than Angelica how to motivate the men, but Yorick seemed so enraptured by his newly acquired knight that he didn't even notice.

"You'll have to see to your own investiture," the alchemist grumbled. Probably he could have found someone to give Angelica her arms, but since he wasn't allowed to create a new insignia, like he wanted, and proclaim a show of strength to gain its honor, as tradition dictated, he was not feeling very charitable towards the princess.

Angelica, on the other hand, felt better than she had since the day she'd been whacked over the head with a walking stick. "I have a feeling those details will take care of themselves." She leaned against the windowsill and pressed her cheek to the cold stone that separated her past from her destiny. "Is the rigging on this contraption ready to use?" She tugged on the line of wire that disappeared miles away in empty space.

"It probably should be inspected and oiled, an insurance nightmare," the alchemist mumbled, but Yorick knocked him aside, eager to show the princess all he'd learned about the line in the fascinating time he'd spent poking around the alchemist's tower. He had a harness in his hand, a leather thong like a horse bridle, and he held it up for the princess to examine.

"The iron ring here fits into the hook and snaps shut, you see," he said, and fit the ring into the hook, "and then the rider puts the leather harness around the waist here," and as he described how the harness was fitted, he slipped the leather belt around Angelica's waist. She leaned against the harness as she was strapped into place, testing the weight of her body on the thin silver thread.

"It feels sturdy enough," she said, but her words were taken by the wind and lost on the alchemist and the newly acquired squire, because just as soon as the sound escaped the princess's lips, the iron buckle and ring sprang into action as though commanded, and Angelica shot through the tower window like a bullet leaving a gun.

Yorick and the alchemist stood in the window watching her fade to a pinpoint on the horizon. "What do we do now?"

The alchemist shook his head and turned away. It'd happened exactly as he had suspected, all along.

154

CHAPTER FIFTEEN

It took ten minutes to slide all the way down the silver line to the gate of the Kingdom of Prester John, and so it was, roughly ten and half minutes after Angelica first became aware of her quest that she arrived on the steps of its completion. The wire resolved at a decorative arch three feet from the castle drawbridge and dumped her, quite indelicately, at its feet. And by its feet, I mean the feet of a statue so large its big toe was the size and shape of Angelica's head and practically at Angelica's eye level when she stood up and dusted herself off. She tried to make out who it was a statue of, but the thing was so massively tall she couldn't see the stone face almost forty feet in the air on broad stone shoulders above the imposing stone breast plate of a massive knight. She ran her fingers over the stone inscription in the statue's base, but the words had been carved in an alphabet and a language that flowers use, and not one that Angelica knew how to read.

"It took you long enough, didn't it?"

Angelica whirled around so fast the hem of her dress flared around her, like flower petals opening. A man in a long blue robe, leaning on a rickety walking stick, smiled at her with the creases of an ancient age in his eyes. Any fool would know Prester John when he saw him, but as Angelica was a princess, and not a fool, she had to ask. "Prester John," the old monk said, by way of introduction. "And I believe you already know this fellow," and he rapped the statue's big toe with his walking stick.

Angelica squinted up in the blazing sunlight at the statue again, at the ten foot tall earthworm carved into the shield on the statue's chest.

"How did you…" Angelica looked at the feeble old man, his walking stick, and the deserted city that loomed just beyond the castle wall.

Prester John smiled. "You're on a quest," he said. "No time to bother with such trivial questions." He gathered up a fistful of blue robe to stop from tripping over himself as he walked, knocked three times on the gate with his walking stick, and lead Angelica over the draw bridge that yawned open and into the empty city. Angelica followed him, not knowing what else to do. She left the leather harness dangling behind her at the statue's feet.

Angelica followed the old monk through the gleaming white stone passageways of the city, met at each turn of every corner by the blazing white light of the noon day sun. If there was any sound in Prester John's city, it was the constant hum of some mechanism or engine somewhere that hovered just beneath the register of the wind whistling through the deserted courtyards and gables. And at every turn the scent of honey being made: azaleas and tulips, wisteria heavy on the vine, the haze of pollen hanging in the air in late spring. "All the workers must be out seeing to the harvest," Angelica said politely when the monk led her into the same modest kitchen that had once hosted Horace and Geoffrey and Lazarus, and bade her to sit down to the same modest feast.

"No, there hasn't been anyone here for a monk's age." Prester John broke open the bread and offered her half a torn hunk. "Try the oil for dipping, it really is divine."

Angelica politely dipped a small morsel of bread in the oil and popped it in her mouth. A flavor like butter and cut grass blossomed on her tongue. "It really is." She closed her eyes to savor the taste, unlike anything she'd had in Angleterre. "But where does it come from? I mean, you didn't grow and pick the olives and press them all by yourself, did you?"

The monk chuckled and chewed with his mouth open in reply. Then he pushed a basket, folded over and covered by a piece of fine Irish lace, towards her. Angelica pealed the cloth back and found five golden orbs nestled there, waiting. "They're called oranges. And I didn't grow or pick them either."

Angelica picked one up and sniffed it. She had never seen anything like it.

"Go ahead and try a bite." When Angelica tried to bite through the thick citrus skin, the old monk laughed. "Not that way; you have to peel it like a nut." He took the fruit from her and pulled it apart with his fingers, offering her each segment as he freed it from the rind. The fruit tasted like sunshine on the river in late August.

"Then where did it all come from?" she said, after the last morsel had been devoured.

The old monk gestured behind him, through a window

157

that looked out over a modest garden gate. The wall seemed to go on forever, in either direction, just exactly as she'd pictured the wall between Loraine and Angleterre. The monk kicked his feet up and crossed his legs on the kitchen table, watching her with an amused look on his face. "You know what you're looking at, princess?"

"No." Angelica excused herself and went to stand by the window. The humming and buzzing and haze of riotous blossoming came from the far side of the wall, of that she was certain. That bread and oil and things called oranges should come from there as well seemed possible. That forty foot statues of dead heroes should emerge from it, unlikely. "No, tell me what I'm looking at." And then she added, "Please."

"That," said Prester John, "is the Garden of Eden. Everything comes from the Garden, in theory that is."

Angelica heard his words, but she didn't comprehend them. "And I'm to go in there?"

The monk shrugged. "Might be." He uncrossed his legs, took his feet off the table, and grabbed his walking stick to drag himself up from his chair. "No one tells me anything; I'm just the caretaker."

Angelica followed him out into the kitchen yard as he made his way through abandoned, barren melon patches and broken carrot stands towards the imposing, disturbingly modern-looking wall. "But that's where God lives, isn't it?" Angelica felt as if there was no other purpose in living than to be with whatever was waiting on the far side of that wall. She felt as though she could die of longing for it. And the old monk seemed absolutely unimpressed. When they reached the gate he knocked on the iron bars three times with his walking stick as if dropping in on and old friend.

"You go in there and speak to it and tell me if it is God or not when you come out, alright?" He turned away before Angelica even had a chance to thank him. "I'll be around, don't worry. However long it takes."

Angelica watched him hobble away as the iron gate closed, the ivy vines clutching and winding through the cracks in the wrought iron bars as his figure became as indiscernible to Angelica as your face is to a fly. She tried to call out for him to come back, terrified to be alone in this place, but then when she opened her mouth to shout, the sound came out as a fully formed bar of music, complete with high harmonies and low base notes, sheet music floating away from her on the breeze. She grabbed after a dropping base note and held a bar of her words above her in the air before releasing it, like a kite. The notes scattered on the wind and floated away towards the sun.

How bizarre, she thought, but her thoughts didn't form as a voice in her head. Instead they appeared as odd impressions of shapes in her memory that aspirated and then dissipated as a new thought took their place. One of the shapes quivered and then popped. The Tree of Knowledge should be around here somewhere. What would happen if she ate from it? The flowers shivered on their stems and ceased their humming as they all stopped on the same heartbeat. A tear formed in Angelica's eye. It was a terrible sin to eat from the Tree of Knowledge. Everyone said so.

And so Angelica walked. It wasn't difficult at first; whoever tended this endless expanse made sure the pathways were kept clean. Eons passed and Angelica stood directly below the sun that beat down on her from above. It wasn't, however, the strange change in the position of the sun that gave her pause, as it had Horace, but a small glinting glass vial left carelessly in her path. She knelt down to pick it up, and the stopper came loose and spilled out its contents, the scroll unrolling as if by its own mechanism at her feet which was convenient because Angelica was many things, but not a snoop. A title had been stamped across the top of the whisper-thin sheet of paper in bright gold letters. *The Song of Horace.*

Shaking, Angelica sat down on a log in a clearing beside the garden path, one of those overwrought attempts at creating a wild space within the controlled environment that is any decently tended garden, to read the music. The melody was easy to follow but the words were incomprehensible; she knew their definitions, but in their current order and arrangement they made very little sense. She sat waiting for comprehension to come to her, singing the melody softly, trying to puzzle out the connections, and drifted away in her thoughts. What Angleterre needed was a permanent peace, a way to end all invasions for good, so that the councilors and king could get back to their schmoozing and sleeping and granting of lucrative business patents. If anything ever happened to her again, if— say for example, she slipped and hit her head swimming and caught a nasty case of apathy— what would stop the country from falling into ruin?

A wall was the only solution Angelica could think of, but to be effective it would have to be a wall of such infinite lengths as to be confusing, just like the wall around the garden, and how that was to be accomplished she couldn't say. Maybe, she thought, as she casually picked a daisy and tucked it behind her ear, maybe if she ate from the Tree of Knowledge she'd understand how to build it. Maybe she'd think of another solution altogether, one much more feasible than an infinite wall. Maybe…

Angelica sat there thinking about her situation for a long, long time. For several thousand years she sat lost in contemplation, until the decorative ivy and grasses and lichen grew around her and swallowed her up and kept her unable to move. She sat there so long that time came to its end and started all over again, so long in fact that when Horace came into the garden, armed with nothing more than a tune, she was still sitting there.

Hey, I know you! she wanted to call out when she first saw him. He was shorter than she remembered— but the last time she had seen him he was over forty feet tall and made of stone. Angelica struggled against the roots of the plants and tried to free herself to go to him, but the plants held firm; by committee the garden had concluded that the best possible course was to hold Angelica in place. She tried to shout to grab Horace's attention, but an arm of ivy anticipated this thought before it even occurred to Angelica and made itself into a constricting sort of gag: tight enough to choke off her windpipe and prevent any meaningful sound from passing through it, but not tight enough to hurt her, exactly. The plants held Angelica trapped, and so she remained, trapped and silenced, a pair of blinking eyes peering through a striking, princess-shaped bush.

Horace sat down, as he had before, which is natural because it was before when he'd sat down, only the time before before came around again, and all the flowers turned towards him and began to sing, exactly as they had before, and it is resolutely hoped, dear reader, that by now you get the picture: this is just how before works. Horace sat down as he had before, and just like before he unrolled his scroll and sang the notes, and just like before a curious person appeared before him, and whether the person was man or woman it was impossible to say. Angelica watched like the bump on a log she had become. The person floated a bit above Horace, like an angel, but he or she didn't look anything like the stained-glass angels in her father's cathedral.

Although it was hard for Angelica to describe the being when she tried years later, it seemed that the thing stretched open its arms, although it had none, and brought a sword out of the hollow made in space between them. Horace knelt before the being, as a knight would kneel before the king, and bowed his head to receive his investiture as the thing dubbed both his shoulders. To be perfectly honest, a phrase that seldom occurred to Angelica unless she was about to be astoundingly rude, to be perfectly honest it seemed the person was an earthworm.

Angelica blinked, and it was gone.

A millennium passed. On the other side of the universe, a new planet was born. On our side a sun flamed out of existence. Horace sat like a man in a trance, the hilt of the sword pressed to his forehead, until it seemed that they would all sit there waiting for the world to start again and for Angelica to come traipsing in, only to trip over herself, when Horace suddenly stood, stretched, slipped the sword into the hilt on his belt, and turned to look right at her.

Angelica held her breath. She had no idea what would happen if Horace realized that she had been here with him, before, but she suspected it wouldn't be anything good. She closed her eyes, hoping the lichens would cover her eyelids before Horace noticed the bald spot of skin beneath the riotous growth, but she could hear his footsteps coming towards her, and she knew she'd done nothing to dissuade him. She was convinced the gig was up, too, when Horace stopped on the path before her, his knee inches from her ivy-crawling elbow. She opened her mouth to speak, to explain herself and to apologize for eavesdropping, but then she remembered she hadn't any breath. None of it mattered. Horace leaned forward and plucked the flower from behind her ear. Then he turned and walked away.

"Let's see what you have to say about it," he said, and plucked the petals one by one from the flower as he walked away. "She loves me, she loves me not, she loves me, she loves me not..." This of course had not happened before, but Angelica had not been there before to put the flower behind her ear, and so let's just assume everyone in the audience is caught up on this point and move on.

"She loves you!" Angelica tried to shout as he walked away. "Please come back!" but no sound came out. No sound but a terrible rasping the other flowers took for complaining. Count your blessings they started to whisper in the wind, a tune rising up on the humming backs of furious bees. "I will not!" Angelica wanted to scream at them. "I will never see him again!"

163

"Try not to lose sight of why you came here," said a voice on Angelica's shoulder. She couldn't turn her head far enough to the side to see what it was that perched there upon her, which was probably a good thing, as Angelica carried with her a healthy disgust for all things creepy-crawly.

Why did I come here? she cried. Why didn't I just stay home and do my best with what I had? Why didn't I just marry the Duke of Loraine? The earthworm on her shoulder would have smiled at that, but earthworms don't have expressive faces.

Instead, the earthworm shouted: TREE OF KNOWLEDGE, GIVE ME YOUR FRUIT!

Behind Angelica's back— because that's where the Tree of Knowledge was, a nondescript little shrubbery with nothing to divide it from the other plants, not even its microscopic red berries— the Tree of Knowledge lowered one of its shrubby little branches to eye level on the earthworm's face, or where eyes would be if the earthworm had eyes and a face, and the creepy-crawly worm lunged out with its fat, bisected tail and snatched a small red berry from one of the low hanging branches. Open your mouth, Angelica.

Angelica looked, panic stricken, from right to left. Everyone knew that when Eve ate from the Tree of Knowledge she was expelled from the garden forever; at the rate things were going for Angelica, she was certain to be trapped in it roughly just as long. And she wasn't entirely sure this earthworm person was in charge here; wasn't there something about a snake tricking Eve in the first place? Angelica couldn't remember. It had been so long since she'd

164

had anything to eat at all, her thoughts were fuzzy and discon-nected. In the end she decided that yes, she would eat the fruit of the Tree of Knowledge, and not because an earthworm told her to, either. She would do it because it was the only thing she could think of that might give her the answer to the problem facing her country, and that was the only way she could think of to make Horace's death ok. And so she opened her mouth.

When one eats from the Tree of Knowledge, the strangest thing that happens is that one feels absolutely no different than before when one knew almost nothing at all. That is because to know everything there is to know is almost the same thing as knowing nothing. This is because the sum total of all knowledge can be ex-pressed most simply as a sum: $1 + 1 = 2$. Once you eat from the Tree of Knowledge— for, believe me, that point in time comes around eventually for us all— you'll understand what I mean. Until then, you're just going to have to play along. Once Angelica had eaten and realized nothing is really quite so complicated as it seems, she understood why she hadn't been able to break free of the plants that grew around her and over her, and so armed with this understanding she simply stood and shook them off. Then she realized Horace was still alive, somewhere, and so she went run-ning after him. And finally, she realized she did not have to build a wall, because even if a wall could be infinitely long, it could never be infinitely tall or it would block out the sun, and then she felt infinitely stupid, but she didn't let that slow her down because as she ran after Horace she also felt infinitely capable of love.

Horace, she gasped. Horace, wait!

When she finally caught up to him, Horace stopped in his

tracks, turned around, and smiled.

"Why, hello there." He looked down at her which was odd because at five foot nine inches, Angelica was almost a head taller than Horace. "Aren't you a rose among lilies?" Horace smiled again, kneeling, and Angelica grinned from ear to ear. He was alive! But not for long, unless she did something about it.

Horace, please listen, you're in danger. Angelica grabbed her knees to try and catch her breath. Had she been in possession of a human's sensibility at that point, she would have noticed that there were tender green leaves on her knees where her hands should have been, but things look very different to the all-knowing and it complicated the picture for her quite a bit.

"A sapling oak! I know just the place to plant you." Horace bent to pluck her from the ground, but her ankles had taken root and burrowed deep in the few seconds it took to catch his attention. He wrested the roots free, shook the dirt from their tangles, and pressed Angelica between the pages of a slim book he kept in his breast pocket next to his heart. And I know, careful reader, that you are thinking, "Wait, this was before Angelica threw that book at Horace's feet," and you are quite right to point that out, but I would remind you that this before is also after, a mystery it is not for humankind to comprehend.

CHAPTER SIXTEEN

For the first several hours, Angelica screamed her lungs out. I don't know if you've ever heard a baby tree scream, but they have sensational diaphragms in those stick-thin bodies and can really start a riot if the conditions are right. Muffled by the pages of the book, however, Angelica's voice (disadvantaged as it was by being the voice of a human in a tree's body, and not a natural-born tree voice) could barely break through the layer upon layer of paper that held her, pressed flat, near Horace's heart. It did no good. If Horace heard her, if he heard anything at all, then he made no show of it. After the third hour Angelica collapsed, hacking and coughing, against the side of the page pressed next to her face. Another hour more and she was bored enough to try and read what was written there. What else was she going to do to kill time while Horace made his way back to the humble kitchen with the strange monk and the rickety chairs? She pushed her sappy green elbows out as far as she could and tried to make a triangle of her body with the twigs that once were her arms, but it took half an hour or more to wedge the book open far enough that she could actually read the words. So you can imagine her disappointment when she discovered that it was just the book of poetry she'd glanced so carelessly at before and thrown just as carelessly out the window.

This is what the poem said:

…when the places in our mind are spaces filled

(here the poem begins with an ellipses because the page pressed against Angelica was not the first page of the poem, and since she couldn't turn the pages, she had no idea how many verses lay before it)

> …when the places in our mind are spaces filled
> by turning worms, then you and I will meet.
> You will not recognize my face,
> and you, grown old from years of care,
> may think a trace of sorrow lingers
> where you once bent to kiss my brow,
> but I am yours, both then and now…

And on and on like that it went. It was doggerel. She read it over again, and a third time, just to be certain she hadn't skipped any clues as to what the poem was about. When no clues were forthcoming, she sat back and read it over a few hundred times more anyway because there wasn't much else to do in Horace's pocket, and it kept her mind off the gnawing hunger that was just beginning to spread itself over her skin. It's a strange sensation to feel the hunger of a seedling when one is used to being human. It's something close to feeling chilly when it's cold.

"Say," she heard a voice booming above her. Horace's voice. "How long was I in there?"

"Twelve minutes," said a second voice, one that sounded so familiar, but then distorted in the peculiar way everything distorted when she became a baby tree, as if all the sounds around her were funneled through a cone around her neck.

"Twelve minutes? Is that all?"

"That's nothing, the girl that went in after you has been in there for half an hour."

"Huh?" That last part was followed by a loud thump and the clang of a flat wooden instrument against an unprotected cranium.

"Pay attention!" The monk hit Horace again for good measure, and Angelica felt woozy as her knight stumbled back and slumped against the garden wall, to keep his knees from giving out.

"Alright, alright, stop hitting me with that thing. What was that last thing you said?"

"I said," Angelica heard Prester John say, and she strained to listen, because she thought the next bit was going to be about how she went in after Horace, but somehow stayed inside longer than he did, even though they'd emerged together, but she was disappointed. "I said, did you get what you came for?"

Horace's shoulder blade moved back and forth. He must have been rubbing his head. "I think so, I mean, there was this woman... or was it a man..."

"What it was isn't important. What matters is what it gave you. A piece of sage advice? Ancient wisdom? New direction?"

"I guess, and a sword." Horace must have shrugged. The

next thing he said was, "I think what it really gave me was another quest."

Prester John laughed. "Well there you go, lad. What more could you ask for? You're a born quester, you might as well have some work to do."

The two men walked away from the garden wall together with Angelica tucked safely into Horace's pocket, and neither of them said a word again until they reached the bottom of the tower stairs. Then Horace turned to Prester John and said, "Have you ever seen it, that thing that's in there?"

"No." Something in his tone told Angelica and Horace both that this was a touchy subject. "Why do you ask?"

"Well, it seems the farther we move away from the garden wall, the more indistinct my impression grows about the thing. And I have the strangest suspicion that it wasn't human."

"Then what pray tell do you believe it was?"

"Please don't hit me again, but... I think it was an earthworm."

Prester John leaned on his walking stick, smiled at the sunshine, and said something very strange. "The whole world is contained in the most humble living thing," he said. The strangest thing about it was that it made perfect sense to Angelica; from her vantage point between the pages she could see that what he really meant was $2 - 1 = 1$. But then she started thinking in shapes again and the whole thing fell apart. Prester John's walking stick dug into the dirt. "Come on, we're late for dinner."

Horace and Angelica climbed the tower stairs, and reunited with Geoffrey and Lazarus, and left the kingdom of Prester John, and Geoffrey was swallowed by the lake monster, and Lazarus was spat upon by a demon snake and ran away in the Desert of Unfathomable Nightmares, all more or less as it had been before, except for Lazarus, naturally, and except for the little cabin of the strange couple that lived on the edge of the Forbidden Forest. When they reached that spot in the journey, Horace on foot and Angelica between the pages of a book, the squat, grumpy cabin was on fire.

"Geoffrey's Uncle! Geoffrey's Aunt!" Horace rushed towards the burning cabin with his sword drawn, if only because it was the final remaining vestige of his knighthood, and that is if you don't count the princess-in-plant-form that he carried close to his heart. His heroics did no good. That the cabin had burned for several hours was clear; the walls shuddered to smoldering and the windows had broken out like teeth, the dying flames only occasionally licking the roots of the remaining panes. No sound came from within save for the irrational crackle of wooden logs breaking apart. If anyone had been inside when the structure caught fire, they were there no more. Horace slumped against the eaves of the round front door, providing the final push needed to send the structure crumbling to shambles. He threw his sword aside. The cross-shaped metal instrument clattered against a pile of discarded metal breast plates scattered at the foot of a nearby tree.

The reader will kindly remember that it wasn't until after Horace's visit to Geoffrey's family, sans Geoffrey, that he obtained his golden, earthworm-etched breastplate. Without his armor he stood absolutely no chance of being taken seriously by the alchemist, let alone Yorick, the squire waiting for him to come along just a ways down the road. He had something he didn't have the first time around– Angelica– but then 1) he wasn't aware of that, and 2) Angelica's absence from the capital city meant that the possibility of her hand in marriage no longer distracted the land-poor, ego-rich Duke. In short, and skipping over the dry and frustrating vagaries of time travel, the Duke of Loraine had attacked.

Horace figured this out—that the Duke had attacked, not the vagaries of time travel—roughly the same time we did, when his sword clattered against a brass breastplate with a strange woman's face molded into the abdomen. He only had to look at it twice to notice the snakes winding from the woman's head, curling under the breastplate's prominently sculpted muscles, and highlighting the depth of the façade of a belly button. As anyone could see, the Green Knight of Loraine's one valley, the Valley of Disappointing Songs, had fought there, and fallen. Where his body had gone was anyone's guess.

At any rate, there was no sign of Geoffrey's family.

Horace sat down against a tree facing the courtyard where the Uncle made his first suit of armor, and tried to cry. He began with one of those sobs of frustration that starts with the urge to release pressure, a half choked whimper. Horace made this crying-type noise until his body caught up with his voice and the real tears started to flow; they eeked out against the corners of his eyes, stinging the sand and the wind-burned, red lipped skin there, and licked the rough tanned skin of his lower eyelids before tipping over the edge and landing in fat, raindrop-sized splotches on his dung-heap knees. And then they began in earnest.

Angelica listened. She pressed her face against the Horace's-heart side of the book, and stroked the page there with her leaf. "If I could comfort you, I would," she whispered. Then she closed her eyes and wished that she could comfort him, for lack of any better action. As it turns out, a wish was all it took.

Horace reached into his vest pocket around the same time or a little after Angelica made her wish. He pulled out the book and let it fall open, hoping to find an answer or some sort of direction. What he found there was a flattened sapling tree, the one that had chased him out of the garden, although that memory seemed to make less and less sense the farther he strayed from the wall. He plucked the miniature tree from between the pages of the book, and the plant stretched and shook its tiny branches in the wind.

Horace had seen enough by then to know when he was in the presence of magic. Carefully, oh so carefully as not to disturb a single leaf, he laid the fragile seedling in his lap and scratched out a hole in the dirt beside him with his stubby fingers. The roots of the plant were, for the most part, still intact, and so it wasn't much strain on Horace's imagination to come up with the plan to try and replant it. When the stem drooped against his foot, Horace saw that he'd have to prop the plant up somehow, and grabbed his sword to make a stand for the tree and plunged it deep into the earth so that only the handle and a few inches of the blade remained above the surface. "Stay there," Horace said, and he ran into the thicket to fetch some water.

Angelica felt her spine stiffen against the cold metal edge as her roots dug into the rich soil, and then the most peculiar thing happened. She began shedding her budding leaves. "Oh no!" she cried, and clutched at the bald place where her head used to be, certain this meant that once the enchantment was broken she would have no hair. She watched in horror as green, copper-edged leaves gathered at her feet and gnarled, fat roots broke the surface of the soil and then dove down through the loam and rock again. Her back arched and snapped, it seemed of its own accord, and then she started to grow. She grew until she was taller than the sword Horace had propped her against, swallowing the weapon in her oaken girth, and then, almost as suddenly, she was taller than the trees of the Forbidden Forest. Taller, and more ancient in appearance, than any tree on earth.

When Horace came back with a discarded helmet upended and sloshing with water, he tripped over one of Angelica's massive roots and dropped everything at the foot of the mighty oak that had so recently appeared there. The seedling was nowhere to be found, and while Horace didn't remember the oak tree having been there before, or even before before, he was far enough out of the garden to think that because it was there, it must have been there all along. And so he picked up the helmet, wiped the water out from inside the metal hull, and looked around for his sword for a while until he finally saw it, protruding from a sap-dripping break in the trunk more than thirty feet above him. Horace cursed and kicked the trunk for a few healthy minutes, bewildered by the strange misfortune of returning with the intention of watering a seedling only to find his sword stolen by a full-grown tree, and then went on his way to the capital, leaving Angelica behind.

The life of a tree is a good, long life, but for Angelica it seemed especially dull and dreary. She could do precious little but watch from her high place all the destruction that the Duke of Loraine's forces had inflicted on her kingdom in the time she'd been away – how long had it been? A day? A year? A lifetime? She shook the thought from her head and a murder of crows took flight from her branches and went cawing and skittering out into the evening sunlight. If only Horace would come back, she thought.

Horace, at that very moment, had crossed the threshold of the Forbidden Forest and was stumbling through the knights that lay strewn across the battlefield. "Once I reach Angelica," he thought, "and make her love me…" although he couldn't see, as he sloshed through this waste of war, what good it would do to win the love of the princess, never mind what the earthworm told him. Anyhow, it was too late. The battle raged ahead of him at the eastern wall of the castle, and as he made his way towards the gate, he fell in with a marching column of the Duke of Loraine's men for cover. He kept his head down, pretending to be the approaching enemy. It was the only way he could think of to reach the castle unimpeded. He tried not to think about what he would have to do to get beyond the gate.

"Horace! Horace Dungpeddler!" As it turned out, it wasn't much. When he reached the trenches along the eastern wall, a squire laden down with blood-stained swords and chainmail shirts came clomping up to him, panting under his heavy burden and shuddering at each volley of arrows over their heads. "Don't you recognize me?" Horace helped the lad with some of his burden, still trying to blend in with the Duke of Loraine's men, and so he was surprised to find that behind the wall of rust red cloaks

175

and daggers was Horatio Dungpeddler, his cousin and childhood friend. His face was still the same ruddy red moon, half terrorized by the crop of carrot red hair that sprouted out at odd angles beneath his helmet, and it was plain his love for war had not abated. "Horatio? What are you doing on this side of the battle?"

The two young men carried the pile of dirty weapons along the front line, holding tight to the castle wall to avoid being struck by one of the iron maces or pots of boiling water that occasionally streamed down the side from the hand of one of Stupid King Mark's holdouts high above them.

"What, is this your first day in the war?" Horatio gave Horace the side-eye. Horace had, in fact, been fighting this war all his life, and many other people's lifetime's to boot, but he made no mention of that as he stepped over the body of a young man that had been propped against a wooden load-bearing wall. It was Yorick, dead from an arrow wound and a few other unfortunate scrapes, but since Horace met Yorick in his first return to the kingdom, and not before leaving it, he didn't notice.

"I've just returned from the quest," Horace stammered lamely.

"Well you're too late, they gave up the quest ages ago." Horatio knelt beside a cistern where water trickled into a wooden basin and then ran in rivulets through the trenches of dirt on all sides. "Here, help me wash these."

Unsure what else to do, Horace took the blade to wash in the basin, following Horatio's example. The weapon cleaned, he stacked it on the pile that Horatio started, and as they worked the pile grew and grew. The battle raged all around them, but if the Duke of Loraine's men suspected they were from the other side, not one of them stopped to ask about it.

What about the princess? Horace wanted to ask, but when he opened his mouth a scream broke his concentration. High above them a man slumped to his knees, a cough of blood on his lips, and fell over the wall to his death. Horatio stacked the last bit of armor to be washed in a neat pile beside the basin, covered it with an old bit of burlap, and trudged towards the fallen knight. Come on and help me with this, he gestured. Horace followed him, not sure what they were meant to do with the vacant body. Horatio, on the other hand, seemed weary of cleaning blood off swords and collecting the wasted bodies of men. When he reached the dead man, he hunkered casually behind him, clasped the man about the waist, and pulled him to his feet as if shepherding a drunk.

"Help me with his feet," he grunted, and Horace grabbed the dead man's feet. Together they lifted him above the muck of oil and blood that sloshed to mud about them, and carried him across the battlefield, to what purpose Horace knew not. All around him men screamed their dying breaths, and the setting sun stained the sky blood red in sympathy, but nothing stopped the fighting, not even their procession through the battlefield and across its front line. Soon Horace and Horatio were behind the castle gate, and the man's body, safe with a few others of its kind, could be forgotten.

Within the castle was more chaotic than without, if that can be imagined. Courtiers and elegant society women shouted down each other in frustration and horror as each volley of

177

flaming arrows set something new on fire. Stupid King Mark still held court in his throne room— why would something as destructive as war make any difference to someone who did absolutely nothing?— but other than that, everything about Angleterre had changed. Horace followed Horatio as he pushed his way through the shoving, sobbing mass of court people, wondering what on earth he was meant to do next. "The Duke's men do terrible things to the knights they capture! Think what they'll do to the women!" A woman in a scarlet wig, set slightly askew on her head, touched her neck.

"Where is the princess?"

Horatio shrugged, drew back a plain tapestry covering a section of wall in a deserted hallway, and pushed open a low, squat door hidden behind it. He pointed for Horace to squat down and crawl through it first, perhaps because he was the shorter of the two. "No one knows. She vanished about a week ago, and it's been chaos ever since the Duke of Loraine got wind of it."

Horace climbed into the passage on his hands and knees. There was a grate at the end of the tunnel, a light shining through it. He looked back and Horatio shoved him forwards. "Some people say, and this is just between us now," Horatio's voice echoed through the tunnel and rang in Horace's ears, "but some people say: what's the use in fighting if the princess isn't coming back?" Horatio whispered this last bit, but it echoed through the tunnel loud and clear. "Isn't the Duke of Loraine the same more or less as Stupid King Mark? Don't tell anyone I said that." Horace reached out to shove the grate open and it swung away from him easily. Horatio nudged him forward, and Horace tumbled through the small opening and into the open air. He was outside again. He was back on the battlefield.

Horace screamed and covered his head with his hands as one of the knights of the Duke of Loraine lunged at them with an axe, but then the terrible warrior seemed to realize mid-chop that they were not knights, only lowly squires, and so he turned his attention to some more worthy target. Horace and Horatio were left to gather up the weapons and armor they'd cleaned on the previous trip, and so that is what they did. And it was there on the raging battlefield, as Horace pulled a sword from the pile of clean weapons ready to be deployed, that he got an idea that changed the course of history.

CHAPTER SEVENTEEN

"Say," Horace said to Horatio, "I have an idea that might end the war."

Horatio, being a naturally inquisitive chap somewhat tired of the war (for what is a war to a squire but endless cleaning of blood-soaked weapons and the constant search for new employment?) said, "What is it, then?"

Horace held the newly clean sword high over his head as if he'd just yanked it from something with an iron-fast grip, like a stone, and then spoke like he had no idea where the sword came from or how it got there: "I saw a tree in the Forbidden Forest, a very unusual tree. It had a sword protruding from high in the trunk," and here he held the sword as high as he could over his head to mimic the angle of the instrument, "and when I say protruding, I mean it doesn't look so much as though it was plunged there... more like it was already there and the tree grew around it. As if the tree were holding it— do you know what I mean?"

Horatio shrugged his shoulders and went back to gathering up helmets and breast plates stacked on the ground.

"Lots of weird stuff in the Forbidden Forest," the squire said. "If only the princess had never gone there. Oh well, there's nothing that can be done about it now."

"Of course there is, there's always something that can be done. We just have to figure out what it is. Now," but he wasn't sure about the next part; he wasn't sure where the next part came from. Maybe he'd dreamed it or heard it in a fairy tale.

"Now what?"

Horace slapped the final veil of chainmail over his stack of elbow plates and kneecaps. "Well," Horace said, "isn't there a prophecy that a knight will receive his arms from a tree?"

"A prophecy," Horatio scoffed. "Who's stupid enough to care about a prophecy? Not even Stupid King Mark is that thick." Horatio shouldered most of his burden and motioned for Horace to follow as he picked his path through the battlefield, and Horace resisted the urge to shout at the back of his head above the din: YOU DIMWIT DON'T YOU KNOW ANYTHING ABOUT HOW THE WORLD WORKS? HAVE A LITTLE IMAGINA-TION! But he was very glad he didn't, even under cover of the roar of the battle, because to shout such a thing at one's companion when he is only trying to do the best he can with the information he's been provided is very bad form indeed. It wasn't until they'd reached the scullery kitchens of the castle of Stupid King Mark and had been given a slice of bread and half an apple that Horace brought the matter up again, and then all he said was, "I am going to see the alchemist."

Horatio was used to squires and their obsession with the alchemist and all his devices. In his younger days and by this I mean the past year, he himself had fallen victim to the mania that some squires have for knightly displays and shields and emblems, constantly imagining what their own arms will look like once they finally hang in that venerable hall, but he had outgrown that phase and learned to focus on those things which were truly important: clean armor, for one, and alternate routes in and out of the castle, for another. "Go ahead," he said to Horace, "I'm not going to try and stop you."

Horace, like— as aforementioned— any squire in the land, knew exactly where the alchemist's office was, and so, with that, Horace and Horatio shook hands and parted ways. At the bottom of the tower's immense and rickety stairs he did have a pang of regret, for it would have made the high climb much more enjoyable if Horatio were with him to keep him company, just like that day he and Prester John climbed the tower after Horace had emerged from the garden, but then the good monk had been so distant that day, Horace couldn't say exactly if it weren't better to just go it alone. It had been like that the whole journey, he thought, as he set his mind on reaching the summit of the stairwell, one companion after another complaining bitterly that they can't go back to what was on the road behind them. He wondered if it would ever end.

At noon he sat down on the stairwell, about halfway up the tower's impossibly high spiral, and made himself a lunch of a bit of bread left over from his simple scullery breakfast. He heard a noise like the clinking and grinding of rusty gears, and as he popped the last morsel of bread into his mouth, the source of the noise turned on the spiral above him and revealed itself; a knight in full ceremonial armor, slowly making his way down the stairs, because when you are encased in armor, you see, it's very hard to bend your knees. "Going up to see the alchemist?" the knight asked, as he crab-walked his way along the curved wall. "I can't say

I recommend it. He's in an awfully foul mood today."

Horace smiled at the man and thanked him for his advice; what more could he do? He had no intention of turning back. His lunch eaten, he clapped his hands together to try and brush away the crumbs and resumed his climb. At least he didn't have that beautiful suit of golden armor to weigh him down, although I suspect that the wearing of it would have made him that much more credible in the eyes of the alchemist. No matter. The quest had gone very badly for him since he'd reached the Forbidden Forest, the portents, symbols, and foreshadows had been all wrong, and for all the world he wished there was someone about like Prester John to guide him. The slight, thistle-like alchemist in his impossibly high tower would have to do.

At the top of the tower stairs, a black oak door looked down on all who dared to approach. After three loud knocks, as loud as he could manage since the clapper was a good foot and a half above his head, the door slowly creaked open. On the other side, the alchemist stood with his back to the entrance, looking out the enormous window, alone. He didn't, if he was aware of it, acknowledge Horace's existence.

"Please sir," Horace said, but too timidly, and his voice was taken by the wind that whistled through the alchemist's chamber. "Please sir," he tried again, this time with more confidence and heft. The alchemist turned and regarded him, a steaming cup of tea in his hand, the bored look of very important personages on his face. "Please sir," Horace said, a final time, "there's been a fantastic discovery and the Red Knight sent me here to tell you of it." That last part, of course, was a lie, one of the justifiable kinds you use for expedience, and really, Horace could rationalize that it was true. It was the Red Knight's refusal to join the quest that sent him down the road that eventually brought him here, so it wasn't a lie really.

The alchemist raised his eyebrow like a fastidious man delicately extending his foot to step over a mud puddle. "A discovery? Is it the whereabouts of the princess?"

"No," Horace said, and something about that struck him as wrong although he couldn't explain what exactly. He tried to put it out of his mind and focus on the tree, which was the heart of the matter, for the moment. He held his hands high over his head to try and illustrate the immensity of the fantastic oak. "Or, well, you see Sir, a tree grows in the Forbidden Forest, an ancient tree although I dare say no one has ever noticed it before…"

"Tosh," the alchemist said, and turned back towards the window. "Once a day some squire is up here with a story about a tree no one's ever noticed before. They're a dime a dozen, lad."

"Yes, but this tree," Horace said, almost hopping up and down to get the alchemist's attention again, "this tree has a special feature surely someone would have noticed before this point— you see, there's a sword growing from the tree. It's growing from the tree's heart."

The alchemist turned then, and looked at Horace, as if the man before him had just then popped into existence, which is what Horace had been counting on since he'd started climbing the stairs. "Growing from the tree's heart?" the alchemist said. He set down his tea cup and lugged a large book bound in dusty leather from the bookcase packed with volumes behind his desk. "That strikes a chord, doesn't it?" He was friendly now, almost jovial, and when Horace looked over the alchemist's shoulder as he thumbed through the foxed and crinkled pages, the alchemist didn't try to put him off. At the center of the book, they found the prophecy.

The alchemist cleared his throat, either from the cloud of mold spores the ancient tome had surely thrown into the air between them as they riffled through its pages, or from a sense of gravity and importance, one can never be certain with old books, and read, "The circle shall be made square. The worm must turn from two to three. The world will be both just and fair when a squire receives his arms from a tree." The alchemist turned the page toward Horace to show him the illustration, the coat of arms of the Kingdom of Prester John with the earthworm etched upon it. Horace had the strangest sensation he had looked at that particular page of that particular book before; modern readers will recognize this phenomenon as déjà vu, but this was well before modern times and the adoption of insightful French idioms, and so Horace only blinked his eyes a bit to keep back the tears that were forming, inexplicably, in the corners of his eyes. "A squire will receive his arms from a tree," the alchemist repeated, and tapped the page. "It's a common formula in prophecy, though scholars always interpret it symbolically, like the snake with the apple in the Garden of Eden; of course there isn't a literal garden, no more than Satan is ever literally a snake..."

Horace thought better than to interrupt the man because he clearly knew what he was talking about and growing more excited by the minute.

"But a tree with a sword in its heart, you did say the sword seemed to be plunged into its heart, didn't you lad?" Horace nodded to encourage the man. "It would be easy enough to establish it hadn't simply been put there by someone, no evidence of sap or other wounded material in the bark," he went on mumbling, now pulling other books off the shelves and sorting through them. "Gesundheit," he said, after Horace sneezed. "And easier yet to establish the sword can't be removed." He slapped a book down on the desk between them, an illustration from page 309 of T. H. White's 1939 edition of The Sword in the Stone, here collected in the third Appendix of Dixon's Alchemistic Devices and Discoveries Through Time, which lists no publication date. "You did try to remove it, didn't you?" he said, and pointed at the figure of the sword suspended above the unyielding rock that held it fast on the printed page. Horace had to admit that no, he had not, but the alchemist seemed willing enough to forgive him. "Then we will ride there today and see what there is to see. You remember the way?" Horace smiled and was glad to note that at least here he could be of some use. "Excellent. I'll have them saddle my horse. And you can be my squire."

"Thank you sir," Horace said. He didn't think it right to protest that he was a knight already, having received his arms from an earthworm in the Garden of Eden, but then that didn't seem like an investiture the alchemist was likely to recognize legally, since the alchemist was the final deciding vote on such matters and he'd more or less said he didn't believe the Garden of Eden was a literal place, and so Horace followed him, a squire once more, as is the nature of time and fortune.

When they began the long and arduous journey from the

top of the tower to the bottom of it, the alchemist stopped to tug on a thick velvet rope that seemed to run right into the wall and disappear behind it. It made no noise and there was no consequence to the action, but the alchemist seemed satisfied and eager to move on. When they reached the bottom of the tower a horse waited for them, saddled and grazing on lettuce in the garden that stretched along the castle wall. The stable boy handed Horace the reigns. Horace reached out to take them, and the stable boy said, "Ain't you gonna help him up?" and so Horace had to go back around the horse to lace his hands together and boost the alchemist's foot up, higher almost than the two of them could muster, since the horse was more than sixteen hands and between the two of them, Horace and the alchemist, you might have made ten feet if you laid them end to end, but somehow they managed.

"You may lead the way," the alchemist said, a bit prim in his high saddle, and Horace went around the horse again to take the reins. The stable boy looked him up and down as if to say, 'hey aren't you the dung peddler's son?,' but then he looked up at the alchemist, whose judgment was never questioned, and he seemed to decide the best course of action was to give over.

Horace could only laugh; he'd been everything since the quest began, even the one true love of a princess, although he didn't know it, and the first impression he made on this morning was of little to no consequence in the grand scheme of things.
And so it was, on the forty-seventh week and seventh day of the quest, that Horace set out, a squire once again, for the Forbidden Forest.

You may, if you are a careful reader, have been distracted

for the past several pages by a thorny, existential question that often haunts our minds and distracts us from the story when we are reading about time travel, and so, if you'll permit, while Horace and the alchemist make their way to the oak with the sword plunged deep in her heart, I'll try to explain to the best of my ability. How is it, you might ask yourself, that the events that led to the princess's disappearance, a fact clearly accepted by everyone in the kingdom at that moment, seem to have escaped the alchemist's consciousness, or, in other words, why doesn't the alchemist seem to remember the national spectacle that was the tournament and consequent death of Horace? In short, why didn't he pop out of his chair and scream bloody murder when Horace first appeared on his doorstep?

Time is a funny thing. For those of us with only one perspective, it seems to run along a line before and after, never deviating, so just consider, for a moment, that it's possible that somewhere might exist a being with more than one perspective, or many, who may experience time as a combination of lines, a warp and weft, if you will, or for those of you living in the computer age, a network. A network is a jolly good metaphor for what I mean; let's press on with it. If an event is a bit of data on a network, then for the experience to be judged true or false in one's personal timeline, all that need happen is the event be assigned an off or on switch, or as in binary, a 0 or a 1. When the princess left one time and zip-lined, so to say, into another nearby line on the network, some memories previously set to 1 toggled themselves to 0, and so adjusted to the new line. It is a complicated science far beyond my keen, but I hope, in some small way, it clears things up enough so that you can enjoy the rest of the story, which begins here, at the foot of the Princess Angelica, who had, you remember, become the tree with the sword in her heart and the kingdom's last hope for a peaceful resolution to the conflict that tore it apart.

"It's magnificent," the alchemist whispered, awestruck, as he slipped from his saddle.

The tree, the princess, had grown some several feet thicker at the trunk since Horace left her, and her roots gnarled and grunted through the yard, uprooting pumpkins and squash in the garden and leaning heavily in places on the thin, thatch roof, what was left of it after the fire and not that it mattered anyway. The tree was taller, too, much much taller, and Horace noted with dismay that now the sword protruded so far above the forest canopy that he had no hopes of reaching it and trying to withdraw it. The alchemist clapped his hands together like a child. "Have you ever seen a hilt like that?" he gasped. "I believe you're right; that is clearly a sword of extraordinary origins. Boost me up so I can have a closer look." Horace went around into the blacksmith shed and found a step ladder; this he used to climb as far up along the side of the trunk as he could with the alchemist perched on his shoulders. "Oh my," the alchemist said above him, kicking his feet in childlike and inconsiderate glee. "I never thought I'd live to see it. And with etched teeth, just as Catulis described!"

"What's that? Whosit?" Horace tried in vain to twist his head to the side to catch a better look at the operation above him, but he could no more understand what the alchemist was talking about than any of the rest of we poor mortals uninitiated in the alchemistic arts. And so the alchemist went on babbling more or less to himself for the better part of an hour with Horace straining to hold him up. After an hour more beyond that of furious scribbling and note-taking and cross-indexing, the alchemist was at last satisfied of a thorough examination of the sword.

"It is," he said, upon climbing down from Horace's shoulders, "the ceremonial sword of the Order of the Garden." There was something of a fire behind his eyes when he said that and his words were quickly followed by, "I had not hoped to believe it was real."

The tree folded around the sword then, as if hugging it, at least the tree gave the impression that it had folded its long, lovely branches around the gleaming instrument and held it to its heart. In that moment Horace, who could barely make out the features of the uppermost top of the tree as he squinted in the sun that poured into this part of the normally dark forest, had the strange impression that the tree was listening to him. He put his hand gently on the ancient oak bark, but nothing happened, and the alchemist seemed impatient to return to the castle where he could make some proper annotations in the presence of the greatest books ever written, and so Horace had no other choice but to leave the tree be.

And so Angelica sat, rooted to the floor of the Forbidden Forest, a sword confirmed by scholars to be of the Garden of Eden driven into her heart, as the bureaucratic wheels of the capital began slowly turning. "Preposterous!" shouted the men of Stupid King Mark's council when the alchemist presented them all with his findings and made his recommendation for swift and certain action, a new direction for the kingdom, a new dawn of hope for them all. Stupid King Mark, who one would think would raise the loudest and longest objection to the alchemist's plan to overthrow him on the whim of a tree, said nothing at all but sat sleeping on his throne. "There is no clear heir, now that the princess is gone," said another, and the council looked at him as if he'd committed a dreadful social faux pas.

The alchemist, for his part, seemed very happy when he left the council meeting. "Give it some time," he said to Horace in hushed tones as they fled the grand council room for the more inviting tower high above. "They've only just heard and have no idea yet how it might be of benefit to themselves or detract from the plans and hopes of their enemies. They'll come around once they see their own personal advantage in it, a good majority of them, don't worry."

CHAPTER EIGHTEEN

And so it was that three weeks later a faction of the council that believed in a limited government with a bicameral legislature, and saw an opportunity to press their case, came to the alchemist's tower and asked to speak to his squire, for that was what everyone by now had grown accustomed to assuming Horace was. "Squire, we would accept the alchemist's plan," they said to him in the stairway where they'd waited to ambush him with their questions and small requests for favors, "if he could assure us that the man who will be King will be a good man, and committed to democracy, for surely it's past time that our country set aside that ancient and barbaric idea of rule by genetic accident," and they all looked uneasily at one another as they gave voice to these treasons. Horace could only shrug his shoulders, weighted down as they were by two sloshing buckets of water for the alchemist's washing. "What's more," the committee said, "we're willing to accept that the sword is not authentic, but it's of the uppermost importance that the King not discover that, for he has the heart of a child, you know, and it breaks so easily."

Horace nodded, and pushed through the throng of them, and they took this all as his surety and guarantee to press their position upon the alchemist, for they were the sort of men who saw everywhere that which best pleased them, and so they went away saying that the squire of the alchemist was a remarkable fellow, with a firm grasp on the geopolitical situation, and they were in good hands.

The following day Horace opened the door of the eastern tower room with a stack of books to be returned to the King's library and was accosted by a group of courtiers who shouted angrily at him and demanded in harsh and warlike tones his assurance that the King so chosen would not cower before the Duke of Loraine and turn the pride of the country over to the hand of its enemy, but continue the war until the last knight had made the ultimate sacrifice in the cause of freedom, and Horace, who had seen enough knights die since the Duke of Loraine first massed his troops on the eastern border, only looked at them as if they were supremely confused as he shoved past them, but they were all the sort of men who read strength of character and of will in the rudeness of others, and so told themselves that the alchemist's squire was of their number, and determined that the pride of the country would not fall.

The council met that evening, Stupid King Mark snoring heartily at its center as the men discussed the possibility that they might put the fate of the country in the hands of a tree. "We don't even know what kind of tree it is!" one of them complained, and they all agreed in their closely held murmurs that the mind of a tree was inscrutable, far more inscrutable than the mind of Stupid King Mark, and perhaps after all they were better off just letting the war run its course, as horrible as the prospect might seem. And then, out of nowhere, Stupid King Mark woke up. And this is what he said:

"The lad who squires for the alchemist bears the stupid King mark; you should make him your king and be done with it."

194

Then, having said his peace, he fell back to his contented sleep and they all went back to ignoring him.

Of course few things are that easy when dealing with the government of an entire nation, there were forms to fill out and files to stamp, but soon enough the proclamation was made: all squires of the kingdom were invited to attend the investiture of the new king, king to be determined, all rights reserved, not valid in other countries. Flyers were posted and banners were hung, and all throughout the kingdom men were employed to run up and down the cobblestone streets and beyond that even to the houses with no pavement or sidewalk or even reasonable fencing, knocking on doors to make sure everyone had heard the wonderful and terrible news. As the crown was still technically open to anyone, seeing as no one knew who the tree would choose, every knight and lord and father brought his son to the capital for the investiture ceremony, and some even brought their daughters although they arrived several centuries too early for that to be of any use. And so it was that the morning of May 1st came again, as bright and beautiful as it had been the year before, only this time stained by the uncertain year that had preceded it, what with the princess's odd personality changes, her sudden disappearance, and the war itself— and everyone was glad for a fresh spring morning and a new beginning.

Horace spent the night before that second May Day morning kneeling in prayer in the King's chapel, as he imagined all the other squires and knights did to prepare for this momentous day, but in truth most if not all the other candidates found their beds early the night before and caught themselves a good night sleep, eschewing the chivalric traditions for the more modern and fashionable sciences and loudly proclaiming to all that asked why they weren't in the chapels that a good night's sleep was the best preparation for battle, even if that night's sleep was induced by a pitcher or two of the hard grog that flowed freely in the city taverns, and so Horace alone emerged that morning with the creaking knees and half-exhausted, hang-dog look that were the hallmarks of a well-prepared knight. The alchemist congratulated him on his self-sacrifice and self-discipline, two excellent qualities in a leader, and thought to himself that perhaps it wouldn't be so bad if a dung peddler's son were elevated to the monarchy, despite it all. He met Horace at the door of the chapel with a bit of gruel in a warm cup and bade him eat it with the blade of his knife as they walked through the battlefield. "No one can talk of anything else," the alchemist babbled, "and night and day they pester me to know: what manner of man is Horace and what emblem will you choose for his crest?" The alchemist laughed to himself at this juncture, as if he'd made an exceedingly clever inside joke, but Horace was lost in his contemplation of all that had happened and all that was yet to be, and so he neglected to ask the alchemist what he meant, or politely chuckle at his joke, which left the poor man very put out. Luckily, they did not have long to walk and the alchemist soon found companionship more fitted to his station and wit when they reached the clearing near Geoffrey's home and stood in the shadow of the noble tree.

Men from the public works department had come late in the night, as Horace kept his vigil, and built an elegant, festive dais around the base of the tree with a large platform raised at one end where Stupid King Mark and forty or fifty of his most respectable courtiers could sit and watch the action. Many court ladies, those regretfully not invited to sit on the dais with the King, had contrived to build their own viewing box from the ruins of the stable, and had benches brought there from the nearest church so there would be respectable places to sit. They crowded in together now, shrieking with excitement when new friends entered the boxes, shouting to the courtiers they knew on the dais, and exchanging gossip about the strange prophecy and its probable beneficiary. All eyes were on Horace, as impossible as it was to keep eyes on him, with so many taller, stronger men milling about on the forest floor and blocking everyone's view.

You can almost always hear it when a tree wakes; a rustle in the air above seems less the product of the wind than of a vigorous and athletic shake. Angelica shook her branches as she awoke, sending a shower of pollen spores like snow over the spectators and causing most of them to sneeze. Her heart beat fast in her chest, or rather, it constricted: a tree's wooden heart can echo, it can thrum, and sometimes, when it is short-circuited by emotion as Angelica's heart was now when she looked down and saw Horace, it constricts; of all the knights and squires gathered around her trunk that morning, he was the one least likely to be noticed— plain is a word often used to describe him, unremarkable another— but Angelica noticed, and her notice was really the only notice that counted. "I wonder what will happen," she sighed, and her branches creaked and groaned as the wood rearranged itself and settled in again around her thrummy, echoing heart.

It was, as they say in reality television talent contests, the alchemist's time to shine. At his own pre-determined moment, and honestly there was no way of knowing ahead of time when that moment would come, the alchemist stepped down from the gracious viewing box and made his way to the foot of the mighty,

197

magical oak. As the program's beginning had not been published, there was very little fanfare to accompany his procession, so many of the courtiers didn't realize the festivities had begun and went on gossiping and chattering away until the alchemist glared at them altogether a bit more rudely than the situation warranted. This standoff between sound and stare went on for a good few minutes, oblivious as the courtiers were to any but those willing to listen to their stories, and at last Stupid King Mark had to interfere and tell them all to shut up because he was just as anxious as anyone else if not more so that the matter of the leadership of his kingdom be settled. So, for once, he led.

"Thank you, your Majesty," the alchemist said with a deep, officious bow to the king's throne. "And thank you, ladies and gentlemen of the court. We are gathered here today…" and with that, the alchemist launched into the world's most dry and pretentious speech, long and boring and meticulously thought-out, filled with antiquated words like 'thou' and 'irregardless,' conforming strictly to all moral and ethical codes, and utterly devoid of any concrete examples; I mean it was legendary. By the end of it, even Horace, who had learned in his travels always to pay attention to everything, found his thoughts wandering and his heart slipping back to that peaceful garden, that sweet, sunny morning when he first heard the flowers sing.

"And so, without further ado," the alchemist shouted, "let the prophecy be fulfilled!"

They weren't sure, any of them, how such a thing should be accomplished, and when the alchemist cleared off from the foot of the tree with his officious, backwards bowing and his eager piggy eyes, rubbing his hands together as if he expected great riches from the day, one of the established knights shoved his own squire forward with a drunken burp, "Have a go at it, boy," and the rest all queued in behind him with Horace bringing up the rear. That was the one instruction the alchemist had given him: "Give them a good show, let them wonder if it will be you until the very end," the alchemist had said. Horace waited now at the end of the long line of eager, would-be kings, and as he was so short, he couldn't see around them to know what, if anything, was happening to the man at the front of the line. He hardly thought it would present a kingly persona if he tried hopping up and down or bobbing left and right. And so he waited.

Angelica watched in horror. The line of boys, most of them were boys, twelve or thirteen at the oldest— the quest had killed off most of the kingdom's knights of a certain age and many squires had been hastily promoted and just as hastily dispatched in the past year— the line of boys seemed to stretch on forever. "Oh when will we get to Horace?" she thought, anxiously, and although she knew he would win the day intuitively— trees have very well developed intuitions— she couldn't see him because, as you know, Horace was very short. Still she stiffened her trunk and made her branches crane as high as possible in looking for him, and so the first squire who tried to climb her trunk to reach for the sword was thrown off and went about in the crowd complaining that the tree hadn't even given him a fair shot.

Each lad stepped forth in turn, one wearing the livery of the Red Knight, dead though he was and probably succeeded by now by one of the boys that used to sleep on the floor in the big hall with Horace, one wearing the shining garb of the Bristol

Knight, lost in the last timeline and just now resurfacing in the present, one picking on all the others in the loutish manner of the Laughing Knight, who is making his first appearance in this story. Each one in turn stepped to the hem of Angelica's garment, as the poets would later depict it, each spat on his hands, each attempted to climb the trunk of the tree to reach the sword high above them, and each was unceremoniously shaken off as the tree rejected all suitors in favor of the last. It was deliciously dramatic and the court ladies could barely contain themselves as, one by one, Horace came another step closer to his destiny.

And then the moment was upon him. All the other squires had tried, and failed, and faded back into the crowd to whine about their second thoughts and lost chances. Horace could hear them, and tried not to listen, for when he tried to look to the top of the tree, or at least the upper third where the sword protruded, he felt dizzy and sick to his stomach. He didn't need another negative voice to make it any harder to get going. He put his hands over his ears and when that didn't work, he plugged his thumbs into them, which did work, but would make it impossible to actually climb the tree, and he was only beginning to consider his predicament and its solution when Angelica looked down and realized that there was Horace, unobstructed and wholly within her reach, and so she knelt down to embrace him.

Anyone who has watered a tomato plant in the summer sunshine knows that plants move, when they feel like it, with deliberation and purpose, just as swiftly as you or I might move an arm to pick up a cup or throw a book at someone's head. It is rare, however, to see a giant oak tree move, and this one moved with such grace and presence that to see it brought tears to gossipy young courtiers' eyes. Horace, who was the object of this primal and poetic action, choked on a cough that turned terrible on itself like a scream, and then nothing was heard beneath the groaning and creaking of the tree as she folded her arms around Horace.

The hilt of the sword was within his reach. With the calm assurance of destiny and time, Horace reached out now to take it, and everyone cheered as it slipped easily from its oaken scabbard. The cheering was so loud it woke up Stupid King Mark, who looked around himself in annoyance at their obvious joy and relief in his newly appointed successor. He hadn't been so bad a King, he was at that moment thinking, if you count off the last year, which wouldn't have been nearly so bad if not for Angelica's slow disappearance, first in character, then in body, and I draw your attention to King Mark's equivocations and excuses because it was at precisely that moment that something very strange began to happen to Angelica, which is saying a lot if you consider all the strange things that had happened, heretofore, to Angelica, and the cheers of thanksgiving gave way to shouts of horror as it became clear to all that there was a person trapped in the body of the tree.

"I see a face!" one of the court ladies shouted, and, not to be out done, another followed it up with, "I see an elbow!"

"Good God is that a lady's slipper?" one the councilmen screamed from the dais.

Horace, still caught up in the embrace of the tree, what remained of the hulking trunk that groaned and cracked as it split open everywhere around Angelica's emerging body, twisted this way and that, clutching the sword at its hilt high above his head.

"It's a woman!" someone shouted. "Cut her loose!" and Horace, who felt keenly the burden of his crown already, and under great pressure to act with firm resolution in moments of great confusion, hacked indiscriminately at the branches that held him and nearly severed one of Angelica's arms.

The tree was all around her sloughing off, but she couldn't open her mouth, and when she raised her hands to her face to try and feel her lips she turned Horace free and he stumbled backwards, nearly losing his footing against the surge of squires and knights that rushed forward, weapons drawn, to save the lady from the enchanted tree. And if you've been annoyed throughout this story by all the miracles that kept Horace going, be glad at least for this one, for Horace was not killed in the fray.

"The princess!" the cry rose up, as the mass of knights swarming around the oak tree tore away enough bark and hacked off enough wood to free Angelica, each one shoving the one next to get close enough to offer her his hand to try and help her. The courtiers fell all over themselves rushing over the edge of the raised dais, and some fell and ripped their velvet robes and others got mud on their knees and faces, and many said it was the strangest thing they'd ever seen, Angelica emerging from the tree like a lady waking from sleep or a baby being born. "Horace!" Angelica cried out, but her voice was still the whispering shiver of an old oak tree and anyway no one could hear her above the shouting and confusion, and as the throng pressed in around her, Horace was pushed back and forgotten, the sword of Prester John still in his hand.

How I wish that I could tell you that they found one another again. Wouldn't it be lovely to end the story with a wedding?

Wouldn't you like to see Horace put on a well cut suit, flash a confident smile at the audience, and walk out before a congregation of his own subjects in an impossibly high-vaulted sanctuary as if all the world must stop and watch while Angelica makes her way towards him on the arm of Stupid King Mark? There would have been joy for them, and sorrow also, for there can be no joy without sorrow, but think of the babies they might have had, smart, and short, and brave. Oh, if only I could tell you that's what happened. Alas.

This is how the story truly ends: the courtiers and ladies and whatnot thronged in around Angelica, so relieved were they to have her back that they altogether forgot the many machinations they had set in place to solve the problems her predicament created. They insisted Stupid King Mark abdicate his throne that instant in favor of his daughter, and for once the man did something wise for the good of his country. The coronation was scheduled on the spot despite all of Angelica's protests that it was Horace who should be king, and where had he gotten off to? as she hopped on her toes to try and see over everyone crowding around her.

Horace watched for a while from a few hundred yards behind the old cottage as the courtiers and knights hurried Angelica away. It seemed to him all very simple and fitting: now that the princess was restored to them (and he was certain she would be a magnanimous and just Queen) the quest was complete and the dark shadow of the Duke of Loraine would no longer fall on the peaceful little kingdom. Maybe he would go back to peddling dung. He smiled to himself when he thought of his father's patched wooden cart tripping on its creaking wheels through the streets, dropping this or that bit of inventory behind it as it made its way along. It was a respectable enough profession, and would put him in the way of very little magic, of which, he confessed to himself with a chuckle, he had grown quite weary, but still dung-peddling wasn't for him. He knew nothing of Angelica's love for him; how could he? They'd barely spoken this entire time.

And so Horace, being more or less ignorant of the future and his many possible roles in it, waited until the fanfare had migrated west towards Noble Queen Angelica's castle, as it would one day be called, to slip out from his hiding place and into the dark anonymity of the forest, the sword of Prester John still strapped to his waist. As he walked, the small purple flowers twinged with the color of the rising moon still bloomed in the imprint of his foot, but they were smaller blossoms than before and became smaller yet with each step he took away from Angelica's kingdom until they were the evenly spaced, microscopic flowers that bloom in every footprint in every forest, but can't be seen by the human eye, and so no one ever thinks to look for them. He walked until he came to the edge of the Desert of Unfathomable Nightmares, at sunrise, and after a brief rest, he got up and continued to walk.

As he walked, he thought about everything he'd seen and experienced in his unusually long short life, and a strange thought came upon him. What if, he thought to himself, picking his way carefully through the skeletons of the strange lost desert village, everyone lives forever? He didn't mean by his thinking that no one ever dies, of course, for he had seen many men die since the quest had first been announced and he was sure that now that it was over, there would be more deaths yet for him to witness, but what if everyone has their own timeline, and no one ever dies in their own timeline? He'd been in the garden, after all, for eons, but when he came out again Prester John said he'd only been away twelve minutes. And Angelica, she'd been a tree all that time. At least, that's how it seemed to him. Anything was possible.

He worked on his theory all the way through the desert and right up to the edge of the impossibly deep lake where Geoffrey had appeared to die, but what if, it only then occurred to Horace, standing at the edge of the impossibly deep lake and watching the candlelight flicker in the highest windows of the World's Most Beautiful Palace, what if to Geoffrey it seemed that the world split in two and he was thrust to a separate side of it? What if he and Lazarus and the people of the beautiful castle were all there together, thinking Horace was the one who'd died? He sat down on the wreckage of a swan boat, one of many feathered and wooden outcroppings that seemed to form the skeletal mass of all the dunes around the lake, and thought about it. How long was life and what would he do with no quest to work on?

It was a very sad thought, sadder than any Horace had ever had, and he put his face in his hands and wept. He wished he had been able to make Angelica fall in love with him, as the earthworm said he should. Then maybe there'd be something to look forward to. Suddenly he felt a pang in his heart as if he'd done a very stupid thing in leaving home. And it was in this black moment that Constance found him and put her hand on his shoulder.

"You've come back to us," she said, plainly.

Horace looked up at her, not as startled as perhaps he should have been. "I had nowhere else to go," he shrugged.

205

"Come across the lake," she said, and tried to help him to his feet. "There's nothing wrong with you that a good feast won't fix, and a dance or two. I should say by now you've earned it."

Horace nodded, humbly, and allowed himself to be helped, and soon they were across the lake and at the high board, sipping a drowsy wine from golden goblets beneath a portrait of Geoffrey, who grinned above them, ear to ear.

"There's no shame in a comfortable retirement," Constance said. And perhaps there wasn't. In any case, Horace was never heard from in the kingdom of Noble Queen Angelica again.

Angelica was a good and noble Queen, as previously noted, and reigned over her kingdom in good and noble fashion for the remainder of her days, which to everyone else appeared to be sixty three years. Her first act as Queen was to sign a treaty to trade much of the lumber of the Forbidden Forest for fishing and passage rights in Loraine's ample system of rivers, inlets and lochs, which was all the Duke of Loraine wanted in the first place, and an easy enough treaty to negotiate for someone with a good and noble head on her shoulders. In short, Angelica did fine without Horace, her champion, but she never forgot him, nor did she marry, and so at the end of her life she lay alone in her royal bed wishing that things had gone differently all those years ago. Not that she was really alone, for a monarch is never really alone, but it would have been nice to feel a squeeze in her weakening hand from someone who loved her.

Death does funny things to people. When Angelica died, she dreamed she was nineteen again, and walking into the forest with her May Day basket on her arm. She heard something moving on the path ahead, and as she walked deeper into the dark, chilly thicket, she thought she heard the scrape of iron against iron and the clattering of chainmail. On the path before her, flowers bloomed in the footprints of a small man.

For days she followed his footprints, although it seemed he was always far enough ahead of her to be out of her line of sight, even as she tracked him through the desert and in and out of time. When she reached the edge of a lake so deep the water seemed black beneath the surface, she dared not try to swim across. The door of the castle opened slowly and a short man in gleaming golden armor stood there with an earthworm on his chest, waiting for her. In a boat shaped like a swan she went to him, and neither of them ever thought to mention death or time again.

ABOUT THE AUTHOR

Allison McEntire lives in Seattle, Washington. She splits her time between writing, teaching, and learning coding languages. She hopes to one day read this book with her son.